Books

Historical

MacLarens of Fire Mountain

Tougher than the Rest, Book One
Faster than the Rest, Book Two
Harder than the Rest, Book Three
Stronger than the Rest, Book Four
Deadlier than the Rest, Book Five
Wilder than the Rest, Book Six

Redemption Mountain

Redemption's Edge, Book One
Wildfire Creek, Book Two
Sunrise Ridge, Book Three
Dixie Moon, Book Four
Survivor Pass, Book Five
Promise Trail, Book Six
Deep River, Book Seven
Courage Canyon, Book Eight
Forsaken Falls, Book Nine
Solitude Gorge, Book Ten
Rogue Rapids, Book Eleven
Restless Wind, Coming next in the series!

MacLarens of Boundary Mountain

Colin's Quest, Book One,
Brodie's Gamble, Book Two
Quinn's Honor, Book Three
Sam's Legacy, Book Four
Heather's Choice, Book Five
Nate's Destiny, Book Six
Blaine's Wager, Book Seven
Fletcher's Pride, Book Eight
Bay's Desire, Coming next in the series!

Contemporary Romance Series

MacLarens of Fire Mountain

Second Summer, Book One
Hard Landing, Book Two
One More Day, Book Three
All Your Nights, Book Four
Always Love You, Book Five
Hearts Don't Lie, Book Six
No Getting Over You, Book Seven
'Til the Sun Comes Up, Book Eight
Foolish Heart, Book Nine
Forever Love, Book Ten, Coming next in the series!

Peregrine Bay

Reclaiming Love, Book One, A Novella
Our Kind of Love, Book Two

Burnt River

Shane's Burden, Book One by Peggy Henderson
Thorn's Journey, Book Two by Shirleen Davies
Aqua's Achilles, Book Three by Kate Cambridge
Ashley's Hope, Book Four by Amelia Adams
Harpur's Secret, Book Five by Kay P. Dawson
Mason's Rescue, Book Six by Peggy L. Henderson
Del's Choice, Book Seven by Shirleen Davies
Ivy's Search, Book Eight by Kate Cambridge
Phoebe's Fate, Book Nine by Amelia Adams
Brody's Shelter, Book Ten by Kay P. Dawson
Boone's Surrender, Book Eleven by Shirleen Davies
Watch for more books in the series!

The best way to stay in touch is to subscribe to my newsletter. Go to www.shirleendavies.com and subscribe in the box at the top of the right column that asks for your email. You'll be notified of new books before they are released, have chances to win great prizes, and receive other subscriber-only specials.

Angel Peak

Redemption Mountain

Historical Western Romance Series

SHIRLEEN DAVIES

Book Twelve in the Redemption Mountain Historical Western Romance Series

Avalanche Ranch Press, LLC
PO Box 12618
Prescott, AZ 86304

Angel Peak is a work of fiction. Names, characters, places, and incidents are either products of the author's imagination or used fictitiously. Any resemblance to actual events, locales, or persons, living or dead, is wholly coincidental.

Book design and conversions by Joseph Murray at 3rdplanetpublishing.com

Cover design by Kim Killion, The Killion Group

ISBN: 978-1-941786-87-1

I care about quality, so if you find something in error, please contact me via email at shirleen@shirleendavies.com

Description

A past he'd give anything to forget. A haunting guilt he can never make right.
The one woman who held the power to heal his injured soul.

Angel Peak, Book Twelve, Redemption Mountain Historical Western Romance Series

Caleb Covington promised to find and kill the men who'd murdered his fiancée. Seeking peace upon leaving the Union Army to become a Texas Ranger, he turned to bounty hunting after Regina's death. After months of dogged pursuit, killing two of the three men, he'd grown weary of the chase, accepting a deputy job in Splendor, Montana. The peace he sought didn't last long.

May Bacon left the scandal and rumors behind, choosing to become a mail order bride rather than live as a spinster in her New Jersey hometown. Although marriage was her dream, she refused to settle for a union of convenience. Her desire for the tall, charming deputy had her body trembling with excitement, and his request to court her gave May a chance at a future. Her joy didn't last long.

The appearance of a young boy not only stalled Caleb's plan for a future with a woman he cared a great deal about, it brought forth the memory of a past he'd never put behind him. But his past wasn't all that stood between them.

Unusual happenings and dangerous strangers stalk the streets, presenting a risk to more than Caleb and May.

Will the menace sweeping the town push them further apart, leaving their friendship beyond repair, or will it bring them closer as they search for the source of the peril?

Angel Peak, book twelve in the Redemption Mountain historical western romance series, is a full-length novel with an HEA and no cliffhanger.

Visit my website for a list of characters for each series.

http://www.shirleendavies.com/character-list.html

Angel Peak

Prologue

Austin, Texas
1866

Caleb Covington slammed the empty whiskey glass on the bar, glaring at the bartender who held the bottle an arm's length away. "Dammit, Buell. I want another drink. Maybe several."

A sardonic smile appeared on Buell's face. "One more, Ranger man, and that's all you're getting."

Mumbling a string of curses, the reason for his limit on whiskey hit Caleb full force. "Did my captain talk to you?"

The smile on the bartender's face grew wider. "Don't know why you'd think that." Setting the bottle on a counter behind him, Buell leaned on the bar, his features sobering. "I heard you might be planning to meet Sadie upstairs. I'm thinking that's a much safer diversion than burying yourself in another bottle."

"Nothing's safe for me any longer." Caleb held up his empty glass. "One more and I'm done, Buell."

Resting his hands on the edge of the bar, Buell leaned forward, his face devoid of emotion. "You've got to get over this, put it all behind you. Regina's been in her grave almost two years, and you know she wouldn't want you grieving by drowning yourself in drink."

Not many men dared bring up the topic of Caleb's murdered fiancée. Not to his face anyway. The smart ones didn't risk the consequences, especially after he'd finished half a bottle of whiskey. And certainly not so close to the anniversary of her death.

Sweet Regina had been a rare beauty. The daughter of a wealthy rancher, she'd had her pick of suitors. Out of all the men in Austin, she'd fallen in love with Caleb. And he'd fallen just as hard for her. On one glorious, star-studded night, she'd accepted his proposal. Two hours later, her life had been snuffed out by a bullet meant for him.

His features contorted, Caleb slowly raised his head to meet Buell's unyielding glare. "How the hell would you know what Regina would want?"

Buell ignored the question. "You aren't the only one who loved that young woman. She grew up here, brought sunshine to darn near everyone's life. I don't believe there's a single person her bright smile and soft heart didn't touch." Pushing away from the bar, Buell straightened. "So I guess I've a right to give you my opinion. Regina loved you, Caleb, and as sure as I'm standing here, I know she wouldn't want you wasting your life away staring into the dry end of a bottle."

Caleb wished Buell's heartfelt words were a lie. They weren't. One glance from Regina and anybody's day would become better. She had a gift for putting people at ease, ignoring the bad to see only good in everyone. The day she'd sent her light his way had been the most exquisite of his life.

If only he'd stayed away, she might still be alive.

Scrubbing a shaky hand down his face, Caleb swallowed the unending ache of loss. "It should've been me."

Buell knew what he meant. Most everyone who'd known the young couple did. "No one blames you for her death. Not even Big Mike, and he loved that girl more than anything on this earth. Everyone knows he loves and is proud of his son, but Regina?" Buell shook his head, a humorless chuckle escaping. "After his wife died, his daughter became the heart and soul of that man. It's a wonder her death didn't drive him to his own early grave. But it didn't, Caleb. Instead, he kept going because, deep inside, he knew Regina would be sitting on the brightest star in heaven, keeping a watchful eye on him. The last thing Big Mike wants is for his baby girl to think less of him for giving up. And it's the last thing she'd want from you."

Grabbing an already damp rag, Buell wiped off the bar, his own emotions raw after all this time. He'd seen it all, still woke at night to the image of Regina cradled in Caleb's arms, the life seeping from her. A man didn't easily forget such horror.

Throat thick, chest drawn so tight he could barely draw a breath, Caleb set the empty glass down. "They got away with it."

Buell sucked in a slow breath. "Yes, they did. No one's tried harder to find those men than you. And like Regina's death, not one person faults you for not finding those murderous scoundrels. The entire state has been looking for them. Someday, when they're caught, we'll have a grand celebration and your girl will finally be put to rest."

At the sound of laughter, Buell moved to the other end of the bar, pouring drinks for a group of young cowhands. Caleb stared at their faces, the way he did with every unfamiliar face, looking for any sign of recognition. As much as he wanted to believe the killers were still close by, his instincts said otherwise.

He found peace in one of two ways. Whiskey was his salve of choice, but every once in a while, he'd soothe the never-ending ache in Sadie's bed. The irony of the situation hadn't been lost on him.

Regina and Sadie grew up together, fate providing one with a life of love, safety, and wealth. The other had been graced with a drunk for a father and a mother who'd ridden off after Sadie turned ten. Regina reveled in a life few experienced, while Sadie survived by sure determination. Complete opposites, Caleb always thought it a wonder the two had stayed friends. But Regina never gave up on Sadie, praying for a way to tear her friend from the life she couldn't seem to escape.

A year after Regina's death, Caleb and Sadie showed up at her grave on the same evening. He'd been carrying a bouquet of daisies, while Sadie carefully laid one wilting wildflower next to the headstone. It didn't matter. Their sentiments were the same.

He'd been visiting Regina's friend ever since. Sadie was the only one who understood. The only one who offered comfort in a world where none existed. At least not for him.

Forcing himself to turn from the bar, Caleb's weary body carried him upstairs to stand before a door he'd come to know well. Hesitantly, he lifted a hand, stalling a few seconds before giving in and knocking.

He'd almost given up when the door creaked open, his gaze landing on the familiar face with sad, searching eyes. Reaching out her hand, Sadie laced their fingers together, drawing him inside before closing the door on a soft click.

Chapter One

Splendor, Montana Territory
November 1869

Deputy Caleb Covington sipped his punch, enjoying the wedding celebration for his good friend, Adam "Mack" Mackey, and Sylvia Lucero, one of the mail order brides brought to town by several of Splendor's more prominent women. He grinned, remembering the fool Mack made of himself before coming to terms with his true feelings for the black-haired beauty with golden brown eyes.

Surprisingly, Caleb didn't feel the pang of loss at their happiness. After almost four years, he'd learned to live with his fiancée's murder, allowing him to think of a future for the first time since her death. On that thought, his gaze moved across the room to another of the mail order brides. Curvy, with wavy, flaxen hair and light blue eyes, his attention centered on her rosy and quite kissable lips.

"I don't know what's stopping you."

Caleb's attention jerked to see Mack standing beside him. "Stopping me?"

Chuckling, Mack tilted his glass toward May Bacon. "You've been interested in her for months. Don't you think it's time you considered courting her?" Caleb's lack of response didn't deter him. "There's no better time than right now to ask her. I'll walk over with you and retrieve my bride."

A sudden terror tore at Caleb's chest. "Now?"

"Why not? It's not going to get any easier, and you certainly don't want to go through what I did with Morgan Miller...or Dutch, Hex, or—" Mack mentioned the single men of Splendor who would've jumped at the chance to court Sylvia.

Caleb held up his hand. "I understand what you're saying." Sucking in a breath, he finished the punch and set the cup down. "All right."

He took determined strides across the room, stopping within inches of a startled May.

"Oh, Deputy Covington." May flushed, eyes widening.

Swallowing any doubt, he met her confused gaze. "Miss Bacon. I wonder if I could speak with you. In private."

May's eyes lit in surprise before she schooled her reaction. "Of course."

Escorting her to a quiet corner, he settled her into a chair, taking a seat next to her. They sat in silence for several minutes, May watching the way he appeared to battle some unspoken emotions, making her stomach clench.

Shifting in the chair, he let out a ragged breath, then stood. Glancing around the room, he met her expectant gaze. "I'd like to know if you would allow me to call on you."

Lips parting, she stilled, unsure she'd heard him right. "You want to court me?"

His brows furrowed. "Does that come as such a surprise?"

Clasping her hands in her lap, she considered the question. "Not really. I do like you very much, Mr. Covington."

"Caleb."

She offered him a shy smile. "Caleb. But you must call me May."

He liked the way she said his first name. Sitting back down, he pulled one hand from her lap, holding it. "You don't have to decide right now, May. It's a big decision. Consider it for as long as you need."

Staring into his deep blue eyes, May knew she'd be putting off the inevitable. "I don't need time to consider it. Yes, I'd very much like you to call on me."

Eyes twinkling, Caleb squeezed her hand, a relieved smile lifting the corners of his mouth. "That's wonderful." Standing, he helped her up.

Biting her lip, she glanced across the room before gazing up at him. "Would you mind if I let Sylvia and Lena know you've asked to call on me?"

His gaze softened. "Of course not." Placing a hand at the small of her back, he guided May across the room where Sylvia and Mack spoke with Sheriff Gabe Evans and his wife, Lena.

Clearing her throat, May looked between the two ladies, ignoring Mack and Gabe. "Caleb has asked permission to court me. I've agreed."

Gabe sent Caleb a questioning glance, saying nothing. Mack simply grinned.

Lena smiled at Caleb. "That's wonderful." She looked at her husband, then back at the other two couples. "Would it be too presumptuous of me to invite the four of you to our house for supper on Saturday evening?"

Before anyone could answer, the front door opened on a bang. A woman of indeterminable age, bright red hair, and heavy makeup walked inside, holding the hand of a small boy. She'd succeeded in getting everyone's attention.

"I'm looking for Caleb Covington. Is he here?"

Brows scrunched in confusion, he stepped forward. "I'm Caleb Covington."

She tightened her grip on the boy's hand and marched forward, allowing herself a few moments to look Caleb up and down.

"We've traveled a great distance to find you."

Staring at her, he shrugged.

"You were a Texas Ranger, correct?"

He glanced at Mack, then back at the woman. "For a time."

"In Austin?"

"Yes."

"You knew Sadie Moss?"

9

His eyes clouded in confusion. "Sadie?"

"She was a saloon girl in Austin. Do you remember her?"

Pushing aside the dread at her question, Caleb glanced at May before taking a closer look at the boy. His stomach clenched at the blond hair and deep blue eyes gazing back at him. A miniature version of him.

"Yes. I remember her." His voice was low, cautious, and filled with alarm.

Tugging the boy in front of her, the woman settled her hands on his shoulders. "Mr. Covington, this is your son, Isaac."

Caleb stood next to Gabe and Mack, watching Isaac play outside the church with several other children, the women clustered together a few feet away. Two hours later, the shock of the woman's announcement hadn't faded. Nor had the punch of her words.

He had a son. Two and a half years old with the same hair and eyes as his father. The same tentative smile and wary gaze as his mother.

Sadie.

Caleb let out a slow breath, remembering the sweet saloon girl who'd helped him get through the rough time after his fiancée's death. Guilt gripped him at the memory. He'd never said goodbye to the quiet, shy woman who'd been a friend of Regina's. The mental image of her being alone and pregnant with little money caused his chest to squeeze, jaw to tighten. He'd been selfish, his desire for revenge controlling his decisions, leaving the woman carrying his son behind without a backward glance.

After leaving the Texas Rangers, he turned to bounty hunting with one goal in mind. Find the marauders who'd murdered Regina and obtain justice for every innocent they'd killed during their journey of terror through Texas.

He'd never been able to do it as a Ranger. As a bounty hunter, Caleb had found a measure of satisfaction locating two of the men responsible for her death, killing both without a moment's hesitation. The oldest brother, who'd fired the bullet which killed Regina, had gotten away.

After months of chasing the man north, he'd lost him near South Pass City, Wyoming. Low on money, he had no choice but to give up the chase. Caleb rode north to Splendor to work for the man he and fellow Union major, Mack Mackey, had served under during the war. Gabe Evans.

Never in all that time had he even considered the possibility he'd left Sadie pregnant and alone in Austin. If he'd known...

"What are you going to do?"

Gabe's question jerked Caleb from his thoughts of Sadie and the what ifs connected to the memory. Hands clenching and unclenching at his sides, Caleb forced himself to relax, consider a future far different from the one he'd anticipated a few short hours before.

Rubbing his jaw, he chuckled at the sight of Isaac chasing a little girl around a tree. "Isaac will live with me."

He and Mack had shared a small, two bedroom house behind the jail. With his friend's marriage to Sylvia, they'd made an agreement with Noah to move into one of his vacant houses, leaving Caleb to stay in the original house. The one he would now share with his son.

"Any idea who'll stay with him while you're working?"

Caleb winced at Mack's question. He hadn't considered anything other than Isaac having a safe place to live. "None. Guess I'll need to figure something out."

"What about May?"

"No." Caleb didn't question why the decisive response came so easily.

Mack shifted, studying his friend. "I don't know why not. You're planning on courting her."

"Courting isn't the same as asking her to marry me." The stark reality of his words made Caleb cringe. In truth, he couldn't think of a reason the lovely young woman would still want to be courted by a man who just learned he had a young son. The child from a union between himself and a saloon girl. "May has a job. I can't expect her to give that up to watch my son." The last two words came easier each time he spoke them. Realizing his future with May had ended before having a chance to call on her would be harder to accept.

"You might ask Isabella Dixon." Gabe mentioned his wife's closest friend who'd married one of the Pelletier ranch hands. "They live in a house not far from you. With Travis working at Redemption's Edge each day, I'm pretty certain she'd be glad to do it."

Caleb remembered hearing that Isabella had taken care of Gabe and Lena's son, Jackson, when he was Isaac's age. "Isabella would be perfect, assuming she'd be willing."

"She's with Lena and the rest of the ladies. Let's go ask her."

Before Caleb had a chance to consider it further, Gabe and Mack started walking, forcing him to follow. Approaching the group of women, his gaze landed on May.

A stab of guilt sliced through him. Learning they had a child, most men would speed up a courtship, doing all they could to secure a wife, relieving the burden of being a single father. Caleb had no intention of being the kind of man who expected a young woman as lovely as May to take on the burden of a child who wasn't hers.

At this moment, he couldn't think of a reason she'd still want him to call on her. He'd say nothing to May today, though. Getting to know his son, protecting him, was Caleb's only priority and he'd put all he had into it. There'd be time to consider a future with or without May once he and Isaac became comfortable with each other.

"Caleb just needs some time to adjust to being a father, May. I'm certain he'll call on you once he and Isaac have a chance to settle in." Sylvia's heart twisted at the misery on May's face.

"I don't know, Syl. It's been a week without a word from him. When I saw him in the telegraph office on Wednesday, he nodded, then walked out." May clasped her hands together, expression grim. "It's obvious he no longer plans to court me. Learning about Isaac changed everything. You know Isabella Dixon is taking care of Isaac when Caleb works."

"Yes, I heard. She's a wonderful woman and loves children."

May nodded, letting out a disappointed sigh. "I know."

"And she doesn't have a job as you do. It wouldn't have been right for Caleb to ask you to quit in order to watch Isaac." Sylvia took a sip of tea, having no idea what else to say to comfort May. Her friend deserved better than a man who lost interest so easily.

Pushing her chair away from the table, she offered Sylvia a weak smile. "Well, I suppose it's time for me to leave for the Eagle's Nest. Gary Werth, the chef, hates it if anyone is even a minute late." Standing, May picked up her reticule. "Will you be at church on Sunday?"

"Of course. I hope you'll sit with us."

A grateful smile lifted the corners of May's mouth. "I'd love to. I'll see you in the morning, Syl."

Leaving the boardinghouse, May stepped into the crisp early winter afternoon. A slight dusting of snow from the night before had turned the streets soggy, horses and wagons both faring poorly as they moved through the thick muck. Hearing the sound of a child's laughter, she glanced across the street.

Caleb stood facing her, holding a squirming Isaac. She allowed herself a moment to stare before lifting a hand in greeting. When he gave a slight nod and nothing more, she looked away, not wanting him to see her disappointment.

Straightening her back, hurt pulsing through her, May continued to the St. James Hotel. Walking up the steps, she placed a hand on the doorknob, chancing a glance over her shoulder. Her stomach clenched at the sight of Caleb still watching her, a grim expression on his face. This time, she didn't offer any type of greeting. Watching until he turned away, she slipped inside the hotel, shrugging out of her heavy coat as she walked through the dining room to the kitchen.

She'd been considering moving out of the low-level, mundane job of organizing ingredients, preparing potatoes, chopping vegetables, and scrubbing bowls, utensils, and pots.

Back east, before the allegations against her father, she'd worked in an upscale bakery preparing scones, breads, and pastries. Over time, the owner had allowed her to experiment, making recipes customers brought into the store. Most times, May would follow the instructions without adding her own twist. Once in a while, the owner encouraged her to change the ingredients, usually ending up with an incredibly delicious concoction. She had a knack for baking, a talent Gary, the chef at the restaurant, had no interest in discussing.

She wouldn't allow herself to be shoved aside today. May needed no more than ten minutes to present her suggestions for widening their menu, and she was determined the older man would listen.

If he didn't, May would ask for a meeting with Lena Evans, one of the owners. She'd already given her regrets for the supper invitation Lena extended at the reception for Mack and Sylvia. Telling her Caleb no longer wished to court her would be difficult. Lena and Sylvia were the only two people who knew of her attraction to the deputy and how excited she'd been at his request.

Over the last year, she'd learned how fickle men could be and the low odds of finding the perfect match. Sylvia had gone through difficult times with Mack before he'd figured out she was the only woman he wanted.

As much as May wanted Caleb to be the one for her, she couldn't afford to waste time on girlish dreams or men who changed their minds without offering the courtesy of an explanation. The way he'd ignored her today couldn't have been more clear.

Caleb Covington had found a new life with his son. It was up to May to forge a future of her own, forgetting the handsome lawman and the fantasy she'd so completely embraced.

Chapter Two

Caleb sat in his living room, handing Isaac another toy, chuckling each time his son studied the small building block before throwing it back. Stan Petermann had given the set to Isaac the evening he arrived. Each night since, Caleb and his son had spent what seemed hours with the wooden toys. It gave him time to watch Isaac while thinking about May.

"Papa." Isaac dropped a block, rocking back and forth, laughing. The boy's initial caution had lessened each day, as Isabella said it would, and he slept well. Just not in his own bed. Caleb hoped to correct that soon.

As yet, he hadn't cooked a single meal. Lena had contacted several of her friends, preparing a schedule so Caleb wouldn't end up with the same dish each night. He didn't know how long their generosity would last, but he appreciated any help they provided.

A soft, almost imperceptible knock had him walking to the door, keeping his attention on Isaac. Pulling the door open before considering who might be outside, he was shocked to see May, a plate of food in her hands.

Before he could ask her inside, she thrust the plate at him, making no move to enter the house. "I'm sorry about barging in on you without an invitation, but I made these today and thought, well..." She shrugged, peeking around Caleb to see Isaac staring at her. When May gave a short wave, her face softened when the boy raised his hand to wave back. "Anyway, Lena said it would be all right to bring these to you. There's sweet bread, scones, and wild berry tarts." The initial trepidation at appearing unannounced increased when Caleb glanced between her and the pastries, saying nothing. "Well, I should be going." Turning away, she hurried down the steps, stopping when Caleb finally found his voice.

"Thank you, May."

Facing him, she offered a faltering smile before pulling her coat around her and rushing toward the boardinghouse. He stepped outside, watching her disappear. Caleb wanted to call out, invite her inside to spend time with them. Instead, his throat closed, his voice silent.

His shoulders slumped when he closed the door. They'd known each other for months, taking walks, talking about their dreams, and forging a friendship of sorts without actually courting. To Caleb, calling on May was more of a formality, and he suspected she'd felt the same. He might not know if he loved her, but he liked May...a lot.

Shaking off the rush of regret, he bent down when Isaac ran over, feeling a surge of love unlike anything he'd ever experienced.

"Would you like to have one, son?" Eyes wide, his head bobbed up and down. Caleb held out the plate. "You get to pick one tonight. We'll save the rest for later."

Isaac lifted his arm, his little hand snatching one of the tarts. When he rushed back to his spot on the floor, Caleb walked to the kitchen, setting the plate down. Studying each item, he picked up a slice of sweet bread and took a bite. The flavor burst in his mouth, a smile growing on his face. Finishing it in three bites, he lifted another slice. It only took two bites for this one to disappear.

"How is the tart, Isaac?" When the boy twisted to look at him, Caleb almost laughed. His heart lurched at the sight of berry juice smeared all over his face, fingers stained, cheeks bulging. His son's grin left no doubt what he thought of the rich dessert.

Leaning a hip against the counter, Caleb's smile faded. May took the time to bring over a plate of sweets she'd made, sparing no time to talk before rushing off. He wished he knew what it meant. Caleb had been certain she'd have no interest in a man with a young boy. Maybe this was no more than a welcoming gesture. But perhaps it was more. It was his own fault he didn't have an answer.

Placing the dish in the cupboard, he moistened a towel and walked over to Isaac, wiping away the sticky remains from his face and hands. Tossing the rag into the sink, Caleb felt a surge of guilt. No matter the change in his life, the way he'd treated her the last week made him wince. She deserved much better.

Caleb needed to speak with May after church tomorrow, maybe ask her to join him and Isaac for

Sunday supper at the boardinghouse. He'd been a miscreant, hurting a woman he cared about. Caleb hoped May would give him a chance to make it right.

Emerging from the boardinghouse, May kept her head high, refusing to glance across the street at the jail as she made her way down the boardwalk to the church. Caleb's inability to make even small conversation the night before told her all she needed to know.

The shock on his face when he opened the door to see her holding a platter of pastries wasn't faked. He'd been stunned at her arrival, not making even the slightest effort to invite her inside. It seemed obvious Caleb had forgotten all about her.

Glancing behind him, May had seen Isaac on the floor, playing with a group of blocks. It had been a sweet scene. She had no doubt Caleb would be a wonderful father.

"May!"

She stopped, whirling around to see Sylvia and Mack walking toward her. The sight of the newlyweds brought a smile to her face. They were a handsome pair and so obviously in love.

May held her hands out to Sylvia. "Good morning."

Sylvia gripped them, squeezing lightly. "We were going to stop at the boardinghouse."

Before May could respond, the sound of child's laughter drew her attention. Caleb and Isaac were crossing the street to join them.

"Oh my. I forgot something at the boardinghouse." May glanced at Sylvia. "I'll meet you at the church."

Cocking her head, Sylvia lifted a brow. "Are you certain?"

May nodded, already walking away. She felt like a coward, but after last night, she wasn't ready to face Caleb. Her action might appear immature, but the way he'd snubbed her since the wedding, May believed it justifiable.

Hurrying upstairs, she grabbed an embroidered handkerchief, slipping it into the pocket of her winter coat. Checking her appearance in the mirror once more, May left her bedroom at the same time the church bell chimed.

Holding her bonnet down to keep it from blowing off, May rushed toward the church, seeing no sign of Caleb and Isaac. Relief and disappointment warred within her as she entered the front door, forcing her breathing to calm. The four had taken seats in the third row. Even from the back of the church, she could see they'd left no room for her.

"Would you care to sit with me, Miss Bacon?"

Shifting at Hex Boudreaux's familiar voice, a timid smile lifted the corners of her mouth. "That would be lovely, Mr. Boudreaux." Slipping a hand through the arm he offered, the deputy led her to a row on the opposite side and behind Caleb. Sitting, she leaned toward him. "Thank you for offering to sit with me. Does your brother plan to join you?"

Hex and Zeke had arrived in Splendor earlier in the year, both taking deputy positions and making an instant impression on the single women in town. Tall and handsome, May hadn't felt anything for either man, all her attention focused on Caleb.

"Not today. The sheriff has him, Beau, and Cash working. After the shootings and raid on the bank during church last summer, Gabe doesn't want to leave the town unprotected on Sunday mornings."

May nodded in understanding. The raid had left one man dead and others wounded. She opened her mouth to respond, closing it when Reverend Paige entered through a side door.

Settling back against the pew, May cast quick, furtive glances across the aisle at Caleb. Her breath caught when he looked behind him, his gaze landing on her. Unable to hold his stare, she turned to face the front, joining the congregation in the first hymn.

Seeing him glance over his shoulder every few minutes unsettled May, making her squirm in the seat. His apparent interest confused her. Other than the few words they'd spoken last evening, he hadn't approached her since Isaac arrived, giving no indication he still intended to see her. All signs implied the opposite.

"Sit still, Isaac." Caleb whispered the words, settling a hand on his son's shoulder, encouraging him to sit down.

The young boy stayed quiet for less than a minute before climbing onto his knees, turning, and resting his hands on the back of their pew. He smiled at the people sitting behind them.

Hearing muffled laughter, Caleb lifted Isaac, placing him on his lap while taking another glance at May. Sylvia had said she planned to sit with them. It hadn't happened. Instead, May had chosen to attend church with his fellow deputy, Hex Boudreaux. Caleb had nothing against the man. He just hadn't expected the surge of jealousy at seeing the way her shoulder touched Hex's.

Forcing himself to tear his gaze away, Caleb's arms banded around his son, his mind whirling. Each week brought more single men to town, most looking for work, a good number seeking a wife. The thought of May garnering the attention of someone else didn't sit right with him. After all, she'd agreed to allow Caleb to call on her, not any of the other eligible men in Splendor.

He missed walking her to the boardinghouse after work, sharing breakfast on the occasion they both had time, and sitting next to her at church. Mostly, he missed their friendship.

Another wave of guilt assaulted him. It wasn't her fault he hadn't attempted to see her since Isaac arrived. All the blame lay with him.

From the discouraged look in May's eyes when she'd come by his house the evening before, Caleb knew he'd created an incredible mess, unintentionally hurting a sweet young woman. The main reason he'd come to church this morning was to see May, apologize, and invite her to supper. Seeing her sitting next to Hex strengthened his resolve. Caleb had no intention of letting his lapse go unaddressed any longer.

Sliding her hand through Hex's arm, May walked outside, glancing up at a darkened sky. Shivering, she guessed the temperature had dropped ten degrees since entering the church.

"Do you have plans for dinner, Miss Bacon?"

She almost laughed, thinking of the blank pages in her social calendar. "No plans, Mr. Boudreaux."

Hex flashed a brilliant smile, one May felt certain got him most anything he wanted. "I'd be honored to escort you to dinner at the Eagle's Nest." His brows scrunched. "Of course, the boardinghouse or McCall's might be better since you work in the restaurant at the St. James."

Her eyes brightened. "I've only been in McCall's a few times."

"If you agree, that's where we'll go." Movement to his side had Hex turning his head. "Good morning, Caleb."

He looked from Hex to May, his gaze lingering on her. "Morning, Hex." His voice softened. "Miss Bacon."

"Hello, Mr. Covington."

"Miss Bacon and I are having dinner at McCall's. Why don't you and Isaac join us?"

A soft groan left May's lips at the same time a slight grin appeared on Caleb's face. He pulled his gaze from her startled face.

"As long as we won't be interrupting, Hex."

"Not at all. It will give Miss Bacon and me a chance to get to know Isaac."

May stifled the urge to tug on Hex's arm, letting him know she preferred to share dinner just with him. Although she liked Hex and knew she'd have an enjoyable time with him, May didn't want to sit across from Caleb. She needed more time before being in his company for more than a few minutes. Too bad she didn't have a choice.

Caleb shifted Isaac in his arms. "I'm still getting to know him myself." His voice was calm and somewhat teasing as he brushed hair from his son's face.

"Let's get over there before all the tables are gone." Hex tightened his hold on May's arm, leading the group across the street and down the boardwalk to the small restaurant owned by Betts and Elmer Jones. The couple purchased it over a year ago, changing the menu by adding items not offered at Suzanne's boardinghouse. A somewhat rotund woman met them inside, a smile tilting the corners of her mouth at the sight of Isaac.

"I was beginning to think I'd never get to meet your little man, Caleb." Betts ran a hand over Isaac's hair. "Will you all be at the same table?"

Caleb nodded. "We will, Betts."

She glanced around, motioning them toward a table in the center of the room. "Here you are." Setting down a list of what was available, Betts took another look at Isaac, once again ruffling his hair. "I'll get this young'un a glass of milk while you all decide what you want."

Hex handed the list to Caleb. "Gabe told the deputies you're coming back tomorrow. That right?"

He set Isaac in the chair beside him. "It is. Isabella Dixon will be taking care of Isaac."

Caleb slid a look at May, watching as she lowered her gaze, fingers fumbling with the buttons on her coat. She didn't look up, not even when Betts took their orders and brought coffee. When she did raise her head, it was to glance around the restaurant, looking anywhere except at him.

Did it bother May he'd gone straight to Isabella, not bothering to seek her out? Perhaps Mack had been right and he should've asked May if she'd have an interest in watching Isaac when not working. Caleb rubbed his neck. He didn't seem to be doing much right when it came to May.

"Here you are." Betts set plates in front of each of the adults, a smaller one for Isaac. "Let me know if you want more. There's plenty."

Except for Isaac, who chattered away between each bite, they ate in relative silence. Hex asked May a few questions, which she answered with concise replies. She did the same when Caleb drew her into the conversation. Always polite, she gave each man equal courtesy while pushing the food around on her plate. Caleb hated every minute of it. He wanted all her attention on him.

Reminding himself Hex had done him a favor by including them in the dinner plans, he relaxed. They'd have time to talk later, after he put Isaac down for a nap. He just needed to convince May to come by that evening and stay for supper.

A task he realized later would be much harder than he assumed.

Chapter Three

It had been months since she'd chosen the comfort of her bed over a hot breakfast. May pulled the covers snug under her chin, having no interest in leaving the warm bed for the chill of her bedroom. Suzanne kept three stoves on the first floor stoked all night, helping to warm the rooms upstairs. Still, the heat never seemed to be enough to do more than raise the temperature to a tolerable level.

Letting out a slow breath, May sighed in pleasure at the thought of having a day to do whatever she wanted. She'd had Mondays off since starting at the Eagle's Nest, her one day to accomplish errands and perhaps find a quiet spot to read her dime novels.

The meal at McCall's yesterday had been pleasant, even if May did have to endure almost an hour in Caleb's company. Watching Isaac provided a welcome respite. The tiny scamp kept them entertained with his constant chatter, arms flailing when he wanted his father's attention. Which, May conceded, Isaac accomplished with little effort.

When they'd left McCall's, Caleb asked to speak with her. She'd deflected the request with a weak excuse before hurrying back to the boardinghouse.

Sitting next to the window in her room last night, May had picked at a slice of berry pie, sipping coffee she'd let go tepid. After a few hours to think it over, she'd mentally flogged herself for not giving Caleb the few minutes he'd requested.

Lying in bed now, she had to accept her childish thoughts over the last week might not be warranted. Within a few short minutes, Caleb's future had been taken from him when a woman arrived at the wedding reception, gripping the hand of a toddler, a boy who was the spitting image of his father.

The fact Caleb had a son didn't bother May at all. Her heart had swelled at the look in Caleb's eyes when he learned about Isaac. There hadn't been the slightest attempt to evade his responsibilities. Instead, he'd embraced his new role at the expense of anything or anyone else in his life. Including May.

She now wondered how he could've done anything else. Being an instant father forced him to make decisions and approach life in a different way. Still, a part of her hoped he would've included her as he got to know his son.

The woman had brought a small satchel containing a few of Isaac's clothes, a small Bible, and a simple horse figure whittled from a piece of wood. Caleb bought more food, purchased a few toys, and selected additional clothes from the general store.

May couldn't deny it hurt, knowing he'd asked Isabella to help him with all the little decisions, then hired her to watch Isaac while Caleb worked. The friendship between them, although new and tentative, had her believing he might turn to her for assistance.

Instead, he'd chosen Isabella, offering May no more than a terse nod from across the street. Logic told her Travis Dixon's wife was the better choice. Pride and the desire to be near Caleb twisted her thoughts in a way she now regretted.

After several days of painful reflection, May accepted his decisions had been sound. She didn't know if his request to talk had been an attempt to explain his actions, confirm his desire to continue seeing her, or let May know his life no longer held a place for her. The last would be hard to hear, but it would be better knowing his intentions than continuing her silent brooding.

Throwing off the covers, May swung her legs over the side of the bed, making a decision. She knew Caleb would be resuming his duties as a deputy today.

Going through her morning ritual, she dressed, picking a blue cotton dress she knew Caleb liked. Adding a blue ribbon to her hair, May took a careful look in the mirror. Satisfied at her appearance, she slid into her coat, ready to find Caleb.

Caleb resisted the urge to stop by his house to see how Isabella and Isaac were doing. He'd already been by twice that morning. Once to find his son eating small slices of canned fruit, the second hearing laughter as they played a game on the floor. Looking through the window, he'd decided not to go inside and interrupt their fun.

Forcing himself to continue down the boardwalk, he stopped across the street from the boardinghouse, thinking of May. Crossing his arms, Caleb leaned his shoulder against a post, his gaze landing on the front door. He knew she seldom worked on Mondays, using her day off to run errands and do laundry in the tub Suzanne kept behind the boardinghouse.

He thought of checking to see if she was washing her clothes when the front door swung open. His breath caught for a moment, watching as May stepped outside, bundled inside her heavy coat. Stopping at the edge of the boardwalk, she looked around, her gaze passing over him before whipping back to lock on him.

Without thought, Caleb pushed away from the post, a slight smile quirking up the corners of his mouth. He walked across the street, not letting his attention stray from her face. He didn't want her to misconstrue his intentions. Caleb planned to talk with her, and he meant to do it now. Stepping next to her on the boardwalk, he tipped his hat.

"Good morning, May." He saw her slight smile falter a moment before she brightened.

"Good morning, Deputy Covington." Mouth drawing into a thin line, she looked away, as if unable, or unwilling, to say more.

Caleb frowned at the formality. They'd agreed to use their first names after he'd gotten May's consent to call on her.

Was it just a little more than a week ago I'd asked to court her? Caleb shook his head. It seemed like much longer since he'd felt the joy of her acceptance. Then everything had changed when a little boy, the exact image of him, had entered the church, clutching the hand of a woman he didn't know. Everything else in his life had faded away, lost in the sudden responsibility of being a father.

He slid his hands into his pockets. "I wondered if you might have a few minutes to talk. Maybe we could have a meal at McCall's."

May forced herself to remember the reason she'd dressed and hurried outside. She'd wanted to find Caleb, discover if he still wanted to talk. Standing beside him now, she doubted it was a good idea.

Talking wouldn't change the fact he no longer appeared to hold an interest in her. He'd made it plain by not showing the slightest amount of friendship toward her since his son arrived. No matter the change in circumstances, what kind of man shoved aside the woman who'd become a friend, treating her as if she meant no more to him than any other woman he'd known?

May wrung her hands together. As hard as it was to accept, Caleb was no different than her father, a man who cared about her when times were easy and good, ignoring her when conditions changed.

"There's no need to explain anything, Deputy Covington. I understand you have new responsibilities with little time for much else."

Eyes narrowing, nostrils flaring, Caleb wrapped a hand around her arm, leading her down the boardwalk. Ignoring her gasp and wide eyes, he crossed the street, dropping his hold when they entered McCall's. He paused long enough for Betts to nod toward an empty table.

Pulling out a chair, he waited, watching as countless emotions crossed her face before she let out a breath and sat down. Sitting across from her, he ordered two cups of coffee and the dinner special for each of them. Not waiting more than two seconds after Betts walked away, Caleb leaned forward, saying the first words coming to mind.

"I'm sorry, May."

Her eyes flickered. "For what, Deputy Covington?"

A pained look crossed his face. "May, I'd greatly appreciate it if you'd call me Caleb." He waited as Betts set down their coffee. "I'm sorry I didn't come to see you after Isaac arrived."

She rushed to stop him from continuing. "You did see me and didn't show any recognition, as if we'd never met."

Caleb flinched, remembering the day she spotted him with Isaac, raising a hand in greeting. He'd stared, offering nothing in return. It had been a cruel reaction to her kind gesture, the same as the evening she'd brought him a plate of pastries—another act of generosity he'd accepted with no more than a thoughtless *thank you.*

"Something else I'm sorry about, May." He said nothing more while Betts delivered their meals, finding he'd lost his appetite. Instead of picking up a fork, he didn't move, not knowing what else to say.

She lifted one shoulder, her voice softening. "It's all right. Your circumstances have changed. You have Isaac to think about." Picking up a fork, she moved food around on her plate, stomach roiling at the thought of eating anything.

"It's *not* all right, May. You deserve better."

Ice formed in her stomach. Setting down the fork, she clasped her hands in her lap. "Better?"

Jaw clenching, he gave a curt nod. "There are things you don't know about me, May. If you did, a sweet woman such as you wouldn't want anything to do with me."

"Yet you wanted to call on me before Isaac arrived. I don't understand what you're trying to tell me." Her chair scraped against the worn wood floor as she pushed from the table. "If you no longer have an interest in me, just say so. You don't have to make excuses. Believe me, I've heard enough of those to last a lifetime."

Caleb didn't like the way his chest squeezed at what she implied. "Don't leave, May."

Her eyes showed nothing except sorrow. "Do you still have an interest in me, Caleb?"

His hesitation told May all she needed. It wasn't a broken heart twisting in her chest. It was the loss of hope. She could no longer imagine a future with a man she'd grown to like, respect. In time, their friendship might have grown into more, but Caleb didn't seem willing to give them a chance.

"I do want to see you, May. I'm not certain you'll want to spend time with me once you learn about my past."

Stunned at his comment, she leaned forward, resting her arms against the edge of the table. "Before Isaac arrived, were you as worried about your past as you are now?"

"No, I wasn't. Learning about him made me realize we'd never be able to have a future if you didn't know how Isaac came to be, what happened before him."

"Do you honestly believe I'd judge you for your past?"

He snorted a derisive chuckle. "Most people would."

"Well, I'm *not* most people, Caleb Covington."

"No, you certainly aren't, May Bacon."

She pursed her lips, deciding to take a chance most women wouldn't. "I don't have to be at the Eagle's Nest tonight. So, if you're serious about still seeing me..." She let the rest trail off, hoping Caleb would finish for her.

A smile broke across his face. "Miss Bacon, would you care to join Isaac and me for supper tonight?"

"Can you cook, Mr. Covington?"

Brows furrowing, he scratched his chin. "As long as it comes out of a can."

It was her turn to chuckle. "If you supply the food, I'll be happy to cook us supper."

He studied her, relieved they'd come to an understanding.

"While I do, you can tell me about a past so horrible it will change my mind about seeing you."

The relief of a moment before faltered. Caleb knew the sooner she learned of his past, the sooner the gentle, East Coast woman would turn away, focus her attention on a man more suitable.

"It sounds like a good trade to me, May." Picking up his fork, he speared a bit of stew. "Seems my appetite has returned."

Her face brightened as she lifted her fork. "I believe mine has as well."

South Pass City
Wyoming Territory

Chad Devlin sipped his whiskey, his gaze scanning the other men in the tent saloon at the edge of town. Always vigilant, he'd learned not to trust anyone, never allow a stranger at his back. The lesson couldn't be forgotten in the lawless gold town of South Pass City.

For over a year, he'd been hiding in the town populated with some of the most evil men in the frontier. His younger brothers had fallen at the hands of a bounty hunter, all because a stray bullet hit a woman in Austin. Turned out she was the fiancée of a Texas Ranger, the same man who'd tracked and killed his brothers.

More than once, Chad thought the same fate awaited him. When the bounty hunter tracked him to South Pass City, he'd found refuge in a canyon hideaway populated by outlaws only a fool would try to enter alone.

After a few months, word came the bounty hunter had ridden out, giving up the search. But Chad never believed the man had forgotten. No man would forget his woman being murdered by an outlaw.

Tossing back the last of his whiskey, he raised the glass, signaling the bartender. Another drink and he'd ride back to the canyon hideout. He'd been riding with the gang for almost a year, robbing stagecoaches, banks, and the infrequent train. Those were more difficult, requiring them to ride long distances as the railroad didn't come anywhere close to South Pass City.

During this time, they'd lost only one man, their haul totaling in the thousands. Divided up, each member of the gang accumulated enough to live comfortably for years. Too bad none of them could live that life anywhere except in the company of other outlaws.

Wanted posters, determined bounty hunters, and the occasional lawman limited their options. Someday, Chad hoped to ride west, outrun his past, and start over.

He'd heard about San Francisco, a town accepting all kinds of men, no matter their profession or past.

Sipping his second whiskey, Chad allowed himself to think about what he'd been considering for months. He'd heard the bounty hunter who'd killed his brothers had retreated back to Texas, giving up when he couldn't find him.

To be certain, Chad had waited. The time had come to cut his ties with the gang, take his money, and disappear.

Several of those he rode with had spoken of a town in western Montana. He'd heard the territorial capital of Big Pine was large enough to hide without detection and offered plenty of work. Not that he cared about a legitimate job with low pay.

Chad didn't intend to spend more than a week, two at most, before leaving. If the rumors were true about the bounty hunter returning to Texas, he wanted to put as much distance between them as possible. Chad held no illusions about the ex-Texas Ranger. Covington would come for him someday, and he had no intention of ever being caught.

The gang had one more stage robbery planned and another targeting a gold wagon transferring ore from a nearby mine. When those were over and the money split between them, he'd ride north and eventually west. The thriving city on the Pacific Coast called to him. Untamed and populated with those who skirted the edges of the law, it was the perfect spot for an outlaw looking for new opportunities.

Chapter Four

Splendor

"You must tell me all about your supper with Caleb." Sylvia Mackey sat across the table from May, sipping her coffee, glancing over the rim.

Feeling her cheeks heat, May stared down at the untouched stew. "It was wonderful." Biting her lower lip, she looked up. "Caleb is so good with Isaac. Patient and kind. Being a father comes naturally to him."

"And what did you think of Isaac?"

She smiled, remembering the night before. "He's the cutest little boy I've ever seen. And quite smart. When he's not playing, he's talking, or *trying* to talk. Isaac is so full of joy. I haven't laughed so much in a long time."

"Did Caleb explain anything to you?"

May's shoulders slumped. "Between Isaac and fixing supper, we had no time to talk before I had to return to the boardinghouse."

Sylvia wrapped both hands around her cup. "Did he ask to see you again?"

Face brightening, she nodded. "Yes. I don't know when, but I'm hoping we'll have time to talk then." She turned at the sound of the door opening.

Sylvia spoke first, her voice just above a whisper. "It's the new woman from back east." They watched as Betts showed her to a table across the room. "We really should introduce ourselves. She's been in town several weeks and is always alone."

"I wonder what brought her to Splendor. I mean, she's obviously a woman of means. Why would she travel all the way to Montana if not to meet family or friends?"

Sylvia nodded at their empty plates. "If you're finished, we'll introduce ourselves before leaving."

Standing, they straightened their skirts, Sylvia leading the way to the woman's table.

"I hope we're not intruding."

The woman startled at Sylvia's words, glancing between the two young women. "No, not at all."

Sylvia cleared her throat. "I'm Mrs. Sylvia Mackey and this is Miss May Bacon. We've seen you in town but have never had a chance to greet you properly."

The woman's serene expression brightened, eyes flickering. "It's a pleasure to meet both of you. I'm Mrs. Clare Billings. Won't you join me?" The hope on her face had them glancing at each other before Sylvia answered.

"We don't want to impose."

"Oh, it wouldn't be an imposition at all. Please." Clare motioned to two chairs. "Would you join me for lunch?"

May answered. "We've just finished, but I do have time for a cup of tea."

"And you, Mrs. Mackey?" Clare asked.

"Tea would be wonderful."

Clare ordered the drinks when Betts walked over. When she left them alone, Clare looked at them. "I'm sure you must be wondering why I'm in Splendor."

May let a smile tilt her lips. "Well, yes. You see, we both came here as mail order brides." She saw Clare's brows raise at the admission. "Sylvia recently married one of the deputies, Mack Mackey. I believe we saw you at the celebration afterward."

Clare blushed a little. "I know I shouldn't have joined you, but the lively music and laughter drew me to the church. I must apologize for intruding on your wedding day, Mrs. Mackey."

"Nonsense. I'm glad you did. May I be candid?"

Clare nodded. "Please."

"Well, May and I heard you came all the way from Boston. Is it true?"

She waited until Betts set down the cups of tea and walked off. "Why, yes. My husband passed a few years ago. After a time, I became bored with my uninspiring life as a widow." She ran a finger along the rim of her cup. "Since we never had children, I decided to come west."

May's eyes widened. "By yourself?"

Clare chuckled, although a sad expression replaced the serenity of a moment before. "I've learned to do many things alone, Miss Bacon." Straightening her back, she tilted her head. "I'd heard an old acquaintance traveled out here years ago and I hoped to find him."

"Him?" Sylvia asked, a brow lifting.

"Yes. Quite inappropriate, I know. Still, I've been curious about him for quite a long time. Unfortunately, I never had time to reintroduce myself. At breakfast in the Eagle's Nest the day after I arrived, I overheard some people mention he'd left to visit friends. I've no idea when he'll return."

May leaned forward, her voice lowering. "So he *does* live in Splendor?"

Clare let out a shaky breath. "Yes. I saw him the same day I arrived on the stage. Regrettably, I couldn't quite overcome my apprehension at facing him before he took the stage out of Splendor."

"Unrequited love," Sylvia breathed out.

"What?" Clare asked.

Sylvia blushed. "I read about it in one of the dime novels Mr. Petermann orders for Isabella Dixon. When she finishes them, Isabella often offers them to me. So, is he someone you loved long ago?"

"Sylvia," May gasped. "You can't ask Mrs. Billings such a personal question."

A smile appeared on Clare's face. "It's quite all right. Yes, we loved each other many years ago. Now, I'm reconsidering my actions. I acted impulsively by coming all this way without notifying him." She glanced out the window, wishing she'd been more courageous when she first arrived. "From what I've learned, he isn't married, but he may be seeing someone or otherwise committed. Worse..." Her voice trailed off.

"Worse?" Sylvia encouraged.

Clare looked away from the window. "He may not remember me at all."

"I'm afraid that would be impossible, Mrs. Billings." Sylvia and Clare turned their attention to May. "I mean, you're incredibly beautiful and quite nice. It's doubtful any man would forget you." It was the truth. Tall and slender with clear skin and a graceful manner, Clare's dark mahogany hair highlighted with streaks of silver gave her a regal appearance.

"She's right. I can't imagine any man forgetting you, Mrs. Billings." Sylvia touched a finger to her lips. "If I recall correctly, Rachel Pelletier is from Boston. A prominent family. Is your friend also from Boston?"

Clare clasped her hands together in her lap. "Yes, he is. I understand he finished medical school and became a doctor."

May and Sylvia shot surprised gazes at each other.

"Perhaps you know him. His name is Charles Worthington."

The following day, May sat next to Caleb at Suzanne's, taking small bites of quail pot pie. He'd spotted her walking to the telegraph office to post a letter to her father, asking her to join him for lunch. She hadn't expected to spend time with him before church on Sunday. His invitation had surprised and pleased her.

Unfortunately, her thoughts were still on Clare and the reason for her visit to Splendor.

"You're awfully quiet today, May. Are you feeling all right?"

"I'm sorry, Caleb. Yes, I'm feeling fine. I was just thinking about someone Sylvia and I met yesterday."

Pushing his empty plate away, he leaned back in the chair, crossing his arms. "We've had several people arrive in town the last few weeks. Which one are you talking about?"

She chewed her bottom lip, deciding it wouldn't be breaking a confidence to tell him. "It's a widow woman who arrived a few weeks ago. Her name is Clare Billings. She's from Boston."

"The older woman staying at the St. James?"

"That's her. Syl and I have seen her several times, but she's always alone. We introduced ourselves yesterday when we had lunch at McCall's." She took another bite of pot pie. Not wanting to reveal any more, May shifted the conversation to a topic of much more importance. "You still haven't told me about your past."

The smile tugging at Caleb's lips fell, his expression clouded. "Not now." Standing, he grabbed his hat from the seat next to him. "Thank you for joining me, May. I need to get back to the jail. Stay as long as you like."

Stunned, she stared at his retreating back. Forcing herself to ignore the initial anger surging through her, she watched as he left without the slightest glimpse behind him.

Glancing at the other tables, she sighed in relief, thankful no one had noticed the scene. He hadn't raised his voice or done anything to garner unwanted attention. Other than leaving her confused, his actions would've seemed normal to everyone else.

Waiting a few minutes, May slid from the seat, picking up her reticule. She'd been thrilled when Caleb offered to accompany her to work after lunch. The initial elation had turned to distress after he'd left.

Her request to speak of his past shouldn't have surprised him, nor should it have caused such a strong reaction. Caleb hadn't seemed angry. Rather, he'd stiffened, becoming cold and distant.

As she walked along the boardwalk toward the St. James, May couldn't help wondering what about his past distressed Caleb so much. She, and everyone at the wedding, knew Isaac's mother had been a saloon girl. Beyond that, the woman was a mystery. May pondered the depth of his affection for Isaac's mother. *Did he love her?* She had so many questions, not having the right to ask even one.

The woman who'd delivered Isaac to his father disappeared as fast as she'd appeared, leaving no time for Caleb to ask after his son's mother. Then again, Caleb would've already known all he needed. His life in Austin wasn't the mystery to him it was to May.

Climbing the steps to the hotel, she stopped at shouting from the opposite end of the street. Turning, her face brightened. She'd always thought the stagecoach's arrival felt similar to Christmas mornings back home. You never knew who would emerge, what stories they'd share, including their reasons for traveling to Splendor.

She remembered the day of her arrival with the three other mail order brides. Fear, excitement, and hope merged as she'd stepped from the stage. May chuckled at the memory. Life in the small frontier town had been nothing like what she'd left behind in New Jersey. There'd been no friends like Sylvia or men like Caleb. A disillusioned breath left her, mood shifting at the reminder of how he'd left her alone at the table.

Shaking her head, May turned from the stage, then whirled around at the all too familiar bellow of laughter.

"It couldn't be," she muttered to herself, her hand tightening on the stair rail. Taking one cautious step down, she narrowed her gaze to get a good look at an older, slender man of above average height and graying beard talking to Noah Brandt, the blacksmith and owner of the livery.

Her throat tightened, eyes filled with tears as recognition struck. Her steps became faster until she broke into a run.

"Father!"

Dillard Bacon whipped around, a broad smile breaking across his face, arms spread wide. "May, my girl!" He engulfed her in a tight embrace. Pulling away, he caught her shoulders. "Let me look at you. You are a sight, my girl."

She swiped moisture from her cheeks. "What are you doing here? You never sent word of a visit." A gentle cough caught her attention, her gaze landing on a short, squat woman standing next to her father. Next to her stood a young man. Stepping away, May looked between them.

"May, this is Oliver Keenan, my stepson." He sent a warm look at the woman next to him. "And this is Pauline, my wife."

Before May could respond, the woman stepped forward, holding out a hand. "It's so nice to meet you, May. I'm your new mother."

Muttering every bad word she knew, May peeled potatoes for the meals that evening. "Mother," she bit out on an angry growl. She couldn't believe the ridiculous woman actually believed she needed a mother.

It was an unusual occurrence for her to dislike someone on sight, and although May tried to ignore the churning in her stomach, she couldn't find anything appealing about Pauline. It wasn't her appearance, which was frumpy but passable.

The first tick of irritation came when May noticed her mother's brooch pinned to the woman's ample chest. It had been a gift from her father a few years before her mother died. After the funeral, her father had given May all her mother's jewelry, telling her he'd keep it safe until she married. If the pin wasn't enough to sour her toward the woman, she also wore one of her mother's rings and a hatpin.

But something else niggled at May, a vague memory from her life in New Jersey. She'd met Oliver before. She just couldn't remember where or when. May guessed him to be a little older than her. Of average height and weight, his light brown hair didn't set him apart from many men. It was the yellowish hue of his eyes and sallow complexion that triggered the recollection, along with a sinking feeling in her stomach.

Peeling the last potato, she rinsed it in a bucket before setting it on top of the rest. She wished there'd been more time to talk with her father before reporting to her job in the hotel kitchen. After the quick reunion, she'd accompanied them to the hotel lobby, making an apology before hurrying through the restaurant.

Her father, Pauline, and Oliver would be settling into their rooms upstairs. Working today was a blessing. She wouldn't have to face them at supper tonight, but May knew he'd want to spend time with her during his visit. Share meals, maybe take a buggy out to see the area.

Picking up a knife, she cut potatoes, cleaned green beans, and began the dough for rolls, all while wondering why her father had traveled such a long distance with his new wife. He wouldn't make the trip just to visit her. Of that, May was certain. His life back east revolved around breeding and training racehorses, spending all his time at Freehold Raceway or gambling with his friends at local pubs and gentlemen's clubs. There were many who believed him a charlatan, although there'd never been proof of him doing anything illegal.

May acknowledged his animated personality, boisterous with a tendency toward buffoonery at times. As obnoxious as some people found him, he had a big heart and would never maliciously hurt someone.

Still, the rumors of him dealing in fraudulent practices had spread, impacting her opportunities for a good marriage. She'd lost two potential suitors who believed the gossip. Her father's protracted absences and the scarcity of men willing to call on her propelled May to contact Pettigrew's. The letter ultimately resulted in her traveling to Splendor.

No matter how much she disagreed with her father's chosen ways of making money, he was still the man who'd provided for May after her mother died. She just didn't understand his attraction to Pauline. Two women couldn't have been more different.

"Miss Bacon, I need the vegetables."

She whirled to see Gary staring at her, as if it hadn't been his first request. "I have them right here." Hurrying over, she placed the bowl on the counter, then returned to her spot.

May had spoken to Gary about adding her pastries to the menu. As expected, he refused her suggestion, telling her he couldn't chance someone with so little formal training. The following day, she'd made pastries in Suzanne's kitchen, taking them to the St. James for her appointment with Lena. The part-owner of the hotel and restaurant raved about them, assured May she'd talk to Gary, then encouraged her to take the leftovers to Caleb. She still hadn't heard back from Lena, but hoped it would work out in her favor.

Forcing herself to concentrate on her work, she shoved thoughts of family, her job, and Caleb out of her mind. She was already tired and ready for the day to end.

The arrival of her father, his wife, and her son, along with Caleb's odd behavior, had drained away the optimistic mood of the morning. Pounding the dough, shoving hair out of her eyes, May hoped tomorrow wouldn't be more of the same.

Chapter Five

Caleb ran a hand over Isaac's hair, heart clenching as he watched his son sleep. As he did each night when tucking him into bed, he thought of Sadie, how he'd ridden out of Austin, guilt tight in his chest. Caleb had mentioned leaving, but hadn't taken the time to say goodbye on the morning he'd saddled Twister. He hadn't even spared her bedroom window a glance when he rode past the saloon. The memory would haunt him the rest of his life.

Thinking back, he recalled the sadness in her eyes, the way her face fell at the news he'd quit the Texas Rangers to become a bounty hunter. He now believed Sadie knew about the pregnancy when he'd made the announcement. After he left, she had no idea how to find him, where to send a message.

Caleb scrubbed a hand down his face, continuing to stroke his son's hair. He could see Sadie in Isaac's expressions, his sometimes wary gaze. Caleb prayed the boy would have her kind, loving temperament, the qualities his fiancée, Regina, had admired so much.

Holding his hands in front of him, Caleb stared at the backs, then the palms, studying them. As a Union officer during the Civil War, these hands had killed men. He'd drawn Regina into his arms with the same hands, and although they'd never made love, he'd imagined it a hundred times before her death. These hands had

53

stroked Sadie, taken pleasure from her touch, giving back so little.

These hands had held matching Colt revolvers, shooting two of the men responsible for Regina's death. Men who'd begged for their lives. Men he'd ignored as he pulled the triggers over and over.

Lowering his hands, Caleb's gaze shifted to the rough-hewn pine dresser across the room. In the bottom drawer, wrapped in an old blanket, were the two revolvers. He'd planned to use them on the third man. Instead, he'd ridden to Splendor and postponed the hunt, never truly forgetting the man who killed Regina.

Now he had Isaac to consider, and a woman he wanted to get to know better. Caleb let out a weary breath, thinking of lunch earlier in the day.

Even if his words to May weren't cross, the sentiment, his walking out without a backward glance, was inexcusable. She deserved so much better.

But he was a selfish man, and he *wanted* May.

The evening she'd come to the house, played with Isaac while preparing supper, had opened his eyes to all he could lose. He'd seen genuine affection as the two sat on the floor, using the building blocks to create different shapes. Not once had she lost patience or tired of the games Isaac insisted on playing.

He'd planned to walk her back to the boardinghouse, but when the time came, Isaac had fallen asleep to a story May read. She didn't utter one word of complaint at returning to Suzanne's alone.

Closing the bedroom door, Caleb pulled out his pocket watch. May would be leaving work for the boardinghouse in a few minutes. Making a quick decision, he slipped into his coat. Dashing outside to the house next to his, he pounded on the door. Caleb kept his gaze on his own house, impatience growing before Mack finally opened the door.

"Sorry, but is there a chance you or Sylvia could watch Isaac for a bit?"

Crossing his arms, Mack glared at him. That was when Caleb noticed his friend's shirt hanging open and his bare feet. He'd obviously interrupted something.

"Good evening, Caleb." Sylvia stepped in front of her husband, doing her best to smooth her rumpled clothing. "Did you say you need us to watch Isaac?"

"If you have time. I hate to intrude, but May is off work in a few minutes and I'd thought to escort her back to the boardinghouse."

"Of course. We'd be happy to stay with him. Right, Mack?"

He let out a frustrated breath. "If that's what you want, sweetheart."

She clasped her hands together. "Wonderful. Let me get my coat and we'll be right over."

Mack looked at Sylvia. "I need to pull on my boots, then I'll be right there." When she disappeared inside, he leaned toward Caleb. "Your timing is horrible. You owe me."

Wincing, he nodded. "I wouldn't have come over if it wasn't important."

Mack's features softened. "I know."

"All right. I'm ready." Sylvia walked beside him the short distance, striding straight to the bedroom and peering inside. "He's still asleep." She waved her hand. "Go on. You don't want to miss her."

"Thanks, Syl."

Caleb raced outside, running between buildings toward the St. James. Stopping out front, he took off his hat, running fingers through his hair.

He noticed an older couple and a younger man he didn't recognize at a table by the window, sipping coffee and talking. Other than the three, the restaurant appeared to be empty.

Caleb wondered if he should go inside, was ready to take the steps when he saw May. She stopped at the table, speaking to the couple before turning to the other man. After a few minutes, she smiled before turning to leave.

Taking a calming breath, he stood at the bottom of the steps, considering what he intended to say. Caleb had been in such a hurry to get here, he hadn't spared a minute to compose his apology. Hearing the door open, he took the steps up to meet her.

"Hello, May."

She startled, her wide eyes meeting his. "Caleb. I didn't expect to see you." Slipping into her gloves, she peered around him. "Where's Isaac?"

"Sylvia and Mack are with him."

Her brows lifted. "Mack, too?"

He chuckled on a shrug. "Sylvia agreed to stay with Isaac, and Mack said he'd join her." Settling his hat on his head, Caleb stepped next to her, running a finger down her cheek. "I want to say I'm sorry about the way I left you today."

Stilling at his touch, she studied his face, her own a mask. Feet aching and tired beyond reason, she didn't know if she could deal with Caleb tonight.

"Your request to talk surprised me, May." Pursing his lips, he rubbed the back of his neck. "My past is something I've shared with only one other person." He offered his arm. "May I escort you back to the boardinghouse?"

Slipping her arm through his, May smiled, not answering. She noticed Caleb look in the restaurant window.

"Who are the people you were speaking with?" Hearing her groan, his lips twitched. "Are they that bad?"

A humorless snort left her lips. "No, not really. My father arrived on the stagecoach with his new wife and her son."

He stopped, looking behind them at the hotel, then back at May. "The man I saw is your father?"

"I'm afraid so."

He chuckled at the resignation in her voice. "You'll have to explain what you mean." They continued down the boardwalk, Caleb waiting for her response.

"It's a rather long story, and truthfully, I'm too tired to tell it tonight."

The humor Caleb felt a moment before slid away at the complete exhaustion in her voice. "Isabella is taking Isaac to the Pelletier ranch tomorrow and will be spending the night and most of the following day. I'd be honored if you'd allow me to accompany you to supper."

She shook her head. "I can't tomorrow. I'm working in the kitchen again."

"Then I'll take you to lunch."

May lifted a brow at the invitation. "Do you intend to stay through the entire meal?"

He had the grace to look chagrined at the question. "I'll ask Suzanne to pack food. We'll ride out of town and find a private place where we can eat and talk." Slowing their pace, he led her between two buildings. Turning her toward him, he lifted her chin with a finger. "Will that be all right?"

Moistening her lips, she stared into his deep blue eyes. "Yes."

The corners of his mouth slid upward. "Good."

Lowering his head, Caleb brushed a soft kiss across her lips. When she made no move to step away, his arms closed around her, tilting his head to deepen the kiss.

Standing on her toes, May circled his neck with her arms, releasing a quiet moan as intense warmth pooled in her stomach. Her limited experience with the few suitors before Caleb didn't compare to the intensity of his persuasive assault on her mouth. Her reaction couldn't have been more different.

The feel of his lips against hers sent spirals of heat through her entire body. She felt on the verge of melting into him when he raised his mouth from hers. Staring into her passion-filled eyes, he placed one last kiss on the tip of her nose.

Clearing his throat, Caleb let his arms fall away. "I should get you to the boardinghouse." A warm grin tilted the corners of his mouth at the look of satisfaction on her face.

Licking her lips, she lifted her gaze to his, offering a tentative smile.

Taking May's hand, he slid her arm through his, returning to the boardwalk. At the front door, he turned toward her. "Would you like to ride or take a wagon tomorrow?"

A wistful expression crossed her face. "I'd love to ride, but I don't have a horse."

"I'll rent one from Noah."

Her eyes widened. "You'd do that for me?"

Caleb wanted to tell her he'd do much more than rent a horse for her, but it was too soon. They needed to take their courtship slow, make certain May could accept his past and embrace the role of being a mother to Isaac.

"He has a good-natured mare."

She quirked a brow. "Does he have an energetic gelding?"

He studied her as a devastating grin curved his mouth. "I'm certain he does." Glancing around, seeing no one watching, he brushed a quick kiss across her lips. "Tomorrow at noon, May."

"It's so good of you to meet us for breakfast, May." Pauline touched the corner of her mouth with a napkin, then set it back in her lap. She'd been studying the restaurant in the boardinghouse and its patrons with a critical eye from the instant they'd walked in. "The food here is quite good for such an obscure town."

May shot a look at her father, who seemed oblivious to his wife's condescending words. Pauline had made similar comments since arriving. Her son, Oliver, or Ollie, as he preferred, sat next to her in amused silence, not offering his own opinion. Instead, his gaze roamed over May, as if sizing her up. For what, she didn't know, or care.

"Suzanne and her help are excellent cooks." Shifting in her chair, she scooped up a forkful of eggs. Taking her time, she listened to Pauline prattle on about the hardship of their trip, the lack of culture, and dearth of eating establishments in Splendor. Bored, May turned her attention to her father.

"You haven't told me why you made such a long trip, Father. With your work, I'm surprised you could take the time."

He looked slightly uncomfortable, then covered it with a burst of laughter. "Can't a father visit his only daughter? Besides, I wanted you to meet Pauline and Ollie."

"And Lord knows when you plan to return, May." Pauline looked at her husband. "Isn't that right, dear?"

He reached over, patting her hand. "Of course, sweetheart. Ollie was particularly interested in seeing the west. He's a bit of a student of the frontier. Aren't you, Ollie?"

The younger man leaned back in his chair, his gaze still locked on May. "I do find it fascinating."

"He reads everything he can find on cowboys, ranchers, Texas Rangers, Indians." Pauline looked at her son. "Ollie's quite the student."

May stifled a groan. She wanted to ask how long they planned to stay, holding her question when the front door opened. A rush of excitement claimed her when Caleb and Mack walked inside. Without thinking, she waved, motioning them to their table.

Caleb's eyes lit when he spotted her. Saying something to Mack, the two deputies skirted around tables to reach them. To May's surprise, Caleb leaned down, kissing her cheek, eliciting a gasp from Pauline.

"Good morning, May." He looked at the others, remembering the little she'd said about them.

She bit her lip to hide her smile. "Good morning, Caleb, Mack." May looked at the others.

"Who do we have here, my girl?" Her father stood.

Eyes narrowing, Caleb held out a hand. "Deputy Caleb Covington. This is Deputy Mack Mackey. And you are?"

"Dillard Bacon." His voice boomed through the restaurant, garnering the interest of those at the other tables. He grasped Caleb's hand, then Mack's. "My friends call me Dilly. May is my daughter."

Caleb glanced at May an instant. "It's a pleasure, Mr. Bacon."

"Dilly, please." He introduced Pauline and Oliver.

"It appears you know my stepdaughter *quite* well, Deputy." Pauline's disapproving gaze slid up and down Caleb.

Not liking the insinuation, he moved next to May, resting a hand on her shoulder. "May and I are seeing each other, Mrs. Bacon. We've been friends for a while now." He saw the slightest amount of disgust on her face and tension in Oliver's shoulders.

Pauline snickered. "It's quite improper to show affection in public, Deputy. I'm certain your mother must've trained you on proper behavior. And I can't believe May allows your attention in such a personal way. I'd thought better of you, May. Then again, your mother has been dead a long time."

If Caleb hadn't tightened his grip on her shoulder, May might've done something to Pauline, forcing him to put her in jail.

Dillard didn't seem to notice his wife's hurtful words. He looked between Caleb and May. "And your intentions, Deputy?"

May startled at the question, embarrassed at the interrogation and direction the conversation had taken in the middle of the restaurant. "If you'll excuse us, I need to speak with Caleb a moment." Slipping her arm through his, she tried to steer him away. Instead, he held firm, sending a slight glare at each of the three, his voice thick with disdain.

"Welcome to Splendor. I hope you enjoy your stay."

Before they walked more than two steps, Dillard stopped them. "We shall have supper soon, Deputy."

May winced, turning back. "It'll have to be on Monday, Father. That's my night off. I don't know if you'll be staying that long."

Caleb glanced down at May. "We could meet them after church on Sunday, sweetheart." He had no intention of sharing May on her one night off. "Will that be agreeable, Mr. Bacon?"

"Dilly, please. Yes, that will be fine. Fact is, I can't recall the last time I was in a church. I believe we'll join you there."

May ignored the repulsion on Pauline's face. She wondered if his comment meant her father and Pauline married in front of a judge instead of a minister. The thought saddened her. Her mother loved going to church on Sundays, the friendships, potlucks, and socials. It didn't surprise May her stepmother had no interest in those activities.

Caleb placed his hand over May's. "We'll look forward to it, Dilly." Walking to the table where Mack sat, he looked at her. "Do you need to postpone our lunch?"

Her gaze shot to his. "Absolutely not." She glanced over her shoulder, seeing her father watching. "I'm looking forward to riding with you. I just wanted to get you away from Pauline. It wouldn't bother her at all to cause a scene. I'm sorry, Caleb. She had no right to question you."

Gripping her chin between his fingers, he forced May to look at him. "She doesn't bother me. What does is the way she treats you."

"I don't know why I let that woman get to me. It's just..." Her voice trailed off

Caleb's voice softened. "What, sweetheart?"

She shook her head. "She's just so different from my mother. I don't understand why my father married her. When I left New Jersey, there were several wonderful women vying for his attention. Most of them were widows who'd been friends with my mother. Any of them would've been better than Pauline." May sucked in a breath. "Well, it's done. I'm just glad I'll never have to live in the same house as her and Father."

Caleb hoped the same. He didn't know where their courtship would lead, but whatever happened, he didn't want May to be subjected to the woman's venomous behavior ever again.

Chapter Six

May pulled back the curtain of her bedroom window, gazing at the livery across the street. She'd decided to wait in her room for Caleb to appear rather than out in the open where her father, or worse, Pauline, might spot her. After breakfast, she had no desire for a repeat of the uncomfortable conversation.

Knowing the selfish nature of her thoughts, she still wished her father had made the journey alone. Or not come at all.

She could have gone her entire life without meeting his new wife and her son. May understood why she didn't care for Pauline, a woman who would be hard to like. Oliver, though, was a mystery. He said little, but his constant scrutiny made her uncomfortable.

Moving her gaze to the jail, she saw Caleb step outside, taking a quick look up at her window. Spotting her, he smiled, tipped his hat, and strode to the livery. Her stomach churned in anticipation of spending time alone with him.

Deciding not to wait for him to come for her, May adjusted her bonnet, grabbed her reticule, gloves, and coat, then hurried down the stairs.

Retrieving the lunch Caleb ordered from Suzanne, she opened the front door, taking a quick look outside to make certain her father, Pauline, and Oliver were nowhere in sight. Satisfied, she rushed across the street, waving at Noah Brandt and smiling at Caleb as she approached. She handed the lunch to Caleb before turning toward Noah.

The blacksmith and livery owner held the reins of a fine looking horse. "Good day, Miss Bacon."

"Good day, Mr. Brandt." She let her gaze wander over the animal, a grin slipping across her face.

Noah nodded at Caleb. "I heard you need a horse for the day. This is Rooster. He should be lively enough for you." A twinkle appeared in his eyes.

May felt her face heat knowing Caleb had told Noah of her desire for an energetic mount, not a docile one. "He looks perfect."

Stepping next to her, Caleb placed his hands on her waist. "Ready?"

Nodding, she gathered her skirt, feeling another rush of excitement when he settled her into the saddle. Taking the reins from Noah, she stroked the gelding's neck, hearing a soft whinny.

"I believe we're going to get along just fine," she murmured, caressing him again.

Mounting Twister, Caleb held out a hand. "Thanks, Noah. We won't be gone long as I need to get back to the jail. All right if I settle up when we return?"

Clasping the offered hand, Noah nodded. "That's fine. Enjoy your ride."

He watched a moment as they took the trail west out of town, then lifted his face to the clear sky. The air was brisk, requiring warm clothing, but the sky held none of the black clouds indicating snow. They'd had occasional dustings the last few weeks, but nothing major. Perhaps their luck would hold and the winter snows wouldn't begin in earnest for several more days.

Caleb flicked quick glances at May, surprised at her skill. She'd never spoken of riding until he mentioned going on a picnic. From the way she sat in the saddle and held the reins, May had a good bit of experience.

"Where are we going?" Her question dragged Caleb from his musings about her skills.

"There's a creek down the trail a little ways. I thought we could eat there." They rode in silence another minute before he pointed toward a tall mountain in the distance. "The tallest one is Angel Peak. From what I can tell, the snow never completely melts off at the top. I plan to take Isaac on a ride up there come spring. Perhaps you'd like to come along."

May stared at the majestic mountain, her breath catching. Until arriving in Montana, she'd never seen such magnificent ranges. "I'd love to join you."

A few minutes later, the trail split. He took the narrow one heading north, reining to a stop in a tiny clearing. Dismounting, he withdrew the food and canteen from his saddlebag, then shifted to help May down.

"Would you mind bringing the blanket?"

May nodded, untying it from behind his saddle.

"We'll walk from here." He placed a hand at the small of her back, guiding her toward the sound of rushing water.

"Oh, there it is." May smiled up at him before hurrying ahead, stopping at the edge of the creek. "How did you ever find this?"

Setting down the food, he stepped next to her. "I often take long rides after church on Sunday. One day I saw a buck and decided Suzanne might like venison for the restaurant. I lost the buck but found the creek. I've been coming here ever since." He took the blanket from her hands, deciding not to tell her how often he'd thought of inviting her to join him. "Come on. I'm starving."

Caleb ate three Cornish pasties filled with meat, potatoes, and onions before May finished her first. He offered the canteen to her. When she shook her head, he took a swallow before selecting a slice of sorghum cake.

"You aren't eating much." Caleb finished the slice in three bites, grabbing a second.

Offering a small smile, she finished the pasty. Reaching for the canteen, she took a couple sips before lifting a piece of cake and taking a couple bites.

"I've been thinking of my father. It's odd he'd travel all the way out here to see me." She worried her bottom lip. "We exchange letters. Not once did he mention remarrying. I can't help believing there's another reason for them coming to Splendor."

He stretched out on the blanket, resting himself on one elbow. "Isn't visiting his daughter enough of a reason?"

Scrunching her brows together, May shook her head. "My father's never been the same since Mother died. Before I left, he spent almost all his time at the racetrack, in gambling halls, or in gentlemen's clubs. I maybe saw him one night a week for supper, but..." She shrugged, her voice trailing off. "I spent my days riding or with friends, and my nights alone, reading or doing needlepoint."

Caleb waited, seeing her internal struggle. Whatever May had on her mind wasn't pleasant.

Biting her lower lip, she lifted her head. The sadness in her eyes felt like a blow to his gut. Reaching out, he covered her hand with his.

"Before Mother's death, he made a good living breeding and training racehorses. His reputation was impeccable, and his services quite sought after. A horse trained by Dilly Bacon was considered a prized possession in anyone's stable." Her mouth slipped into a grim, tight line. "He lost interest after Mother died, spending more time gambling than with his horses. Then the rumors began."

Caleb lifted a brow. "Rumors?"

"A prominent horse owner accused him of fixing races to settle his gambling debts. It wasn't true, but the accusations continued. He was never charged with any crime, but the rumored scandal hurt what little business he still had. At the time, I had two suitors. Both from prominent families in the racing world." She offered a cynical smile. "Each begged off because of the rumors."

He squeezed her hand, anger building at her treatment by the men who'd professed an interest in her. Jaw clenching, he forced himself to calm down. "Is that why you decided to become a mail order bride?"

May nodded. "As you can imagine, my prospects were limited. I made quiet inquiries and contacted Pettigrew's in Philadelphia. I'd already decided to leave when Father made a decision to turn his fortunes around. He spent his days and nights with the horses, rebuilding his reputation. I didn't see him enough to learn if his efforts were successful. Apparently they were, as I doubt Pauline would be interested in a man without means." She slipped her hand from Caleb's, shifting on the blanket.

"When the invitation to travel to Philadelphia came, I didn't hesitate. I gathered my savings and what belongings I could stuff into one satchel, wrote a letter to Father, and left. He hadn't been home in days, so I don't know how long it took him to learn of my leaving. I didn't write again until I arrived in Splendor."

Sitting up, Caleb moved next to her, settling an arm over her shoulders. He knew it was a bold move, but the pain in her voice, the way her body had begun to tremble, didn't allow him to let her fret alone.

"I'm glad you came to Splendor, May." He leaned over, kissing her temple.

A wistful look crossed her face. "I've no doubt you could do much better than me, Caleb."

"That's far from true, sweetheart." Her admission stunned him. If anyone could do better, it was May, not him. He opened his mouth to explain when he caught a whiff of smoke.

"Do you smell that?" Standing, he turned in a circle.

May jumped up, lifting her face. "Smoke."

"There's a fire somewhere." Grabbing the blanket and leftover food, he gripped her hand. "Come on. We need to find out where it is."

He helped May onto Rooster, tied the blanket behind his saddle, then stuffed the last of the food into his saddlebag. Swinging into the saddle, he led them back the way they came.

"The smoke is getting thicker, Caleb."

Feeling the wind pick up, he glanced over his shoulder, seeing May rub her eyes, heard her choke. He needed to find the location of the fire so they didn't ride into it. Caleb prayed it wasn't coming from town.

The smoke didn't clear when they reached the main trail. The wind swept it one way, then another, making it hard to see from which direction it came.

"We'll head back to town, May. Stay with me. Yell if I ride out of sight."

The closer they came to town, the denser the smoke. Hearing May choke, he tore off his handkerchief, dousing it in water from his canteen. Reining Twister beside her, he held out the soaked piece of cloth.

"Tie this around your face."

"What about you?"

"Don't argue with me, May. You need this more than me." He waited next to her until she'd done as he asked. When she nodded, he turned Twister back toward town, a ball of ice forming in his gut, afraid of what they'd find.

As they rode closer, flames rose from the far end of town.

"It's near the St. James and the church, Caleb."

His stomach clenched at the distress in her words. He glanced up, seeing nothing except clear sky. They could use rain or snow right now.

Racing into town, he pulled up at the livery and dismounted, noting Noah was nowhere in sight. He whirled at the sound of shouting, his gut twisting. The church and community building were engulfed in flames.

"May, stay here. I need to find out what I can do to help."

"But—"

Caleb stepped next to her. "Please. Stay where I know you're safe." He bent, taking her lips in a heated kiss before lifting his head. "I'll be back as soon as I can."

May clasped her hands together, watching him run toward the fire. She hated staying behind, doing nothing.

Grabbing the reins of both horses, she led them into the livery, removing the saddles and tack. Closing the gate behind her, she ran toward the street. She recognized several women carrying buckets, handing wet rags to the men trying to control the flames. Making a decision, she dashed into Noah's blacksmith shop, searching for buckets or anything else capable of holding water. Her shoulders slumped, realizing he must've already taken them.

Shirking out of her coat, May hurried back into the livery, spotting four feeding buckets. Emptying them on the ground, she gripped the empty containers and ran toward the church.

"Over here, May."

She looked up to see Sylvia and Suzanne waving to her. Allie Coulter and Lena Evans were at a nearby water trough, filling buckets. Rushing to them, she handed her buckets to the ladies. In less than a minute, the women had their own brigade lined up, passing buckets to the men.

"May, can you pump more water into the trough?" Lena yelled as she passed a full bucket to Suzanne.

Taking her place across from them, she pumped, her arms straining with the effort needed to fill the trough. Across the street, Abby Brandt, two other mail order brides, Tabitha Beekman and Deborah Chestro, and a couple women from the Dixie formed their own brigade using a second trough to fill buckets.

Gabe dashed up to Lena, his face and hands covered in soot. "The wind is shifting. We need to water down the St. James before it catches fire. Abby's group across the

74

street will keep water moving to the church, but your women need to hand it off to the men next to the hotel."

Lena nodded. "You heard him, ladies. We're passing the buckets to Gabe, Noah, and the men next to the hotel."

May straightened, rolling her head from side to side before gripping the pump handle. Her arms burned at the continued effort, but no one could afford to slow down.

At first, the wind blew south, away from town. The shift turned the wind north, in the direction of the hotel and other wood buildings making up Splendor. If the hotel or Allie's millinery across the street began to burn, the entire town could be lost.

Loud shouts from the north end of town had the volunteers halting for an instant before whoops and hollers erupted. A large group of riders from the Pelletier ranch raced through town to the church, dismounting next to Gabe.

Dax Pelletier motioned for his men to take their buckets and head to the creek behind the church and hotel. In less than a minute, two more brigades were formed.

Eyes burning from smoke, arms and shoulders aching, May continued pumping by sheer will. The feel of a hand on her shoulder had her slowing.

"Let me take over for a bit, May." Caleb stood beside her, gently moving her aside.

Looking around, May watched as the remaining Pelletier men replaced the women at the two troughs. "Only for a couple minutes, Caleb," she choked out. "I'm sure the men are needed elsewhere."

Not slowing the pumping motions, he sent her a tired smile. "We have this for now, sweetheart." He glanced around, his gaze landing on Lena. "Could you, Suzanne, and the rest of the ladies get drinks for everyone?"

Lena nodded, rounding up the ladies. It didn't take long for them to haul lemonade, coffee, and beer outside, passing them around as the men rotated jobs.

"Here you are, Caleb." May handed him a glass of lemonade, heart sinking at the sight of the burned out church. The flames were gone, smoldering embers taking their place. The only damage to the St. James was a few scarred boards.

"We were fortunate, May. The entire town could've been lost." Caleb chugged the lemonade, handing her his empty glass. "Ah hell."

Following his gaze, May's eyes widened. Hex Boudreaux walked out of the charred remains of the church carrying a limp body in his arms. Taking a closer look, she saw it was a woman.

"Oh no!" She ran toward Hex, tears forming in recognition. "Is she alive?"

"Barely. I have to get her to the clinic."

She walked beside him, heart pounding as they hurried along the boardwalk. Doctor Clay McCord ran up to them, wiping grimy hands down his pants. Taking one look at the woman, he raced ahead, shoving open the door of the clinic.

"Place her on the bed in there. I need to clean up."

Hex laid her on the bed while May dampened a clean cloth to wipe the soot from her face, neck, and hands.

Clay stood by the bed. "We need to get the coat off."

"Is she burned, Doc?" Hex asked as he unbuttoned the coat, then lifted her so Clay and May could slide it off.

"Doesn't appear so. I believe she's taken in a good deal of smoke, which can be as fatal." Running his hands over her, he looked at May. "Do you have any idea who she is?"

Biting her lower lip, tears welled in her eyes. "Mrs. Clara Billings. She's from Boston." May lifted her gaze to meet Clay's. "She traveled all the way to Splendor to find an old friend." She shoved aside the lump of pain in her chest. "Doc Worthington."

Chapter Seven

Clay lifted a brow, stilling for an instant in his inspection of Clare's injuries. "Charles didn't mention a friend coming to town before he left." Checking her heartbeat, he looked up. "You two should wait outside. I can take care of her from here."

"If you need me, I'll be helping with the cleanup." Hex nodded at May before leaving.

"I'd like to stay, if you don't mind, Doctor."

Looking up from his examination, he studied her a moment, then nodded. "All right. I could use your help."

"What can I do?"

"We need to elevate her head and shoulders. There are pillows on those shelves." He nodded behind him, then lowered his head, checking her arms and legs.

May hurried to grab them.

"I'll lift Mrs. Billings so you can place the pillows under her. Ready?"

When she nodded, Clay placed his arms under Clare, raising her long enough for May to slide the pillows underneath.

"That's good. Thank you. This should help her breathe a little easier. I'd have you open the front door, but that'll allow more smoke to enter the clinic."

"What else can we do for her?"

Clay pulled Clare's blouse down to check for burns, then lifted her skirt to do the same. "She has some minor burns on her legs, but nowhere else. I can use salve on them. There isn't much we can do about the smoke inhalation, other than make it easier for her to breathe. It takes time for the smoke to clear out of her system. I hope there's no damage to her lungs." Grabbing a chair, he set it next to the bed. "I need to stay and keep watch on her. Thank you for your help, Miss Bacon."

May rested a hand on the bed next to Clare. "I'd be happy to stay with her."

Clay opened his mouth to reply, closing it when Clare began coughing. Lifting her head, he turned her face to the side, patting her back lightly. He glanced at May.

"Get some water."

By the time May returned, Clare's coughing had eased, her eyes opening to slits.

"My throat," she choked out, lifting a hand to her chest. "It hurts."

"You were in the church when it caught fire, Mrs. Billings. One of the deputies brought you to the clinic. Here. Try to take a little water."

Opening her mouth, she swallowed a little, then began another spell of coughing. This one lasted longer, her face grimacing in pain. Pressing a hand to her chest, Clare's eyes widened, then closed, watering in pain. Slowly, the wracking coughs subsided.

Clay settled her onto the pillows, handing the glass to May. "This will go on for quite a while."

"Then you'll need someone to help watch her. You can't stay up all night and work in the clinic all day."

"I can't ask you to give up your time, Miss Bacon. I know you have a job at the Eagle's Nest."

May pursed her lips. "I can come after we close and stay the night. The chef doesn't need me in the kitchen until three o'clock, and I'm off on Mondays. You can show me what to do."

Clay rubbed the back of his neck. "Can you stay with her for a bit while I check to see if there are others injured?"

"Of course."

"We can decide on the rest later. But I do thank you for the offer, Miss Bacon."

May's concerned gaze held steady on Clare. Something about the woman touched her. Maybe it was the fact she'd traveled across country alone in the hopes of talking to a man she'd loved in her youth. Clare hadn't confided the entire story, but it wasn't hard for May and Sylvia to fill in what hadn't been spoken.

Sitting in the chair, she took the woman's hand, holding it in a light grip. Seeing the sallow color of her skin, May felt a wave of anger. She wondered how the fire started, if it was accidental or intentional. The last made her blood run cold.

"May?"

Her heart warmed at the familiar voice. "Caleb." She held out her hand, threading her fingers through his. "It's Clare Billings."

"The woman you mentioned when we had lunch?"

She nodded. "Yes. Doc McCord said she inhaled a lot of smoke. It could be a while before he knows if she'll be all right. I wish Doc Worthington was here."

Caleb looked down at her. "Doc McCord is very competent."

May blinked, understanding his meaning. "It's nothing against Clay. He's wonderful. I think having Doc Worthington here might help Clare heal faster."

"Do you think he means that much to her?"

She let out a breath, nodding. "Yes, I do."

Caleb's eyes narrowed on the woman, deciding he'd ask Clay where Charles had gone.

Squeezing his hand, she tore her gaze away from Clare to look up at him. "Were any others hurt?"

"No. Hex said he found Mrs. Billings outside the back door, as if she'd stumbled from the burning building. He isn't certain, but by the look of the ripped hinges, he thinks she might've kicked the door open."

"Trying to get out?"

Caleb nodded. "We won't know for certain until she's able to tell us."

"How did the fire start?"

Shrugging, he leaned against the edge of the bed. "We don't know yet. Reverend and Mrs. Paige took a wagon out to the Murton ranch this morning, so it's doubtful he'd have left a lantern burning. He always leaves the doors open, so anyone could've come inside and started it."

81

She saw his hard gaze land on Clare. "You aren't thinking she started it, are you? What possible reason could she have for burning down a church?"

Letting out a breath, a muscle in his jaw ticked. "I don't know what to think right now."

The door of the examination room burst open. A disheveled Doc Worthington stopped short, staring at the woman on the bed. He took unsteady steps forward, not sparing a glance at May or Caleb as he approached. Staring down, his breath came in short gasps.

"Clare?" Her name whispered from his lips. When her eyes remained closed, Charles ran his knuckles over her cheek and jaw.

Even with the sickening pallor of her skin and soft lines of age, he recognized her. He'd carried her memory in his heart and mind for years, dreamed about her, never able to give his heart to another woman.

"Clare. Can you hear me?" His gaze moved from her face to glide down her fully-clothed body, seeing the salve Clay had smoothed over the slight burns on her legs.

"The smoke is what got to her, Doctor." Clay stood next to him. "Is she the woman you knew in Boston?"

Shoving aside the pain from their past, he nodded. "Yes." Glancing around the room, he noticed May and Caleb for the first time. "Are you the one who found her, Deputy?"

"No, sir. Hex found her on the ground just outside the back door of the church. It's a miracle she didn't die in the fire."

Squeezing his eyes shut, Charles pinched the bridge of his nose. "Yes, a miracle."

It was all he could think to say. The shock of Clay's news when he'd stepped off the stage began to fade at the sound of Clare's soft breathing. His remorseful gaze met May's and Caleb's.

"I'll stay with her. Thank you both for taking care of her."

Joining Caleb by the door, May looked back at Charles. The prominent lines between his eyes before leaving Splendor seemed to have deepened since his return. "She came to town to find you, Doctor Worthington."

A torrent of sadness gripped him. "Clay told me what you'd said, Miss Bacon. I'm glad Clare met you."

"I know she'll be all right. She has to be." May turned toward Caleb, leading the way out of the clinic.

The following morning, Caleb worked beside fellow deputies Beau Davis and Cash Coulter, probing through the cooled embers of the church. Little remained of the simple building the town had erected before he'd arrived in Splendor. Even with the shock of its destruction, townsfolk were already talking of rebuilding.

"There's nothing here worth saving." Cash shook his head, kicking at another of the blackened boards. "It'd be best to haul it all off."

"I'll bet Silas Jenks has enough lumber for us to get started as soon as Reverend Paige gives his approval." Beau settled fisted hands on his hips, unconcealed disgust on his face. "This is going to be a real blow to him."

Cash pursed his lips, nodding. "He should be back anytime."

The comment had Caleb thinking of his son. Isaac and Isabella were due back from Redemption's Edge sometime this afternoon. He'd been less than enthusiastic when Isabella had mentioned taking him to the Pelletier's to play with the numerous children at the ranch. The chaos of the fire made him thankful he'd allowed Isaac to go.

The night before, he and May had eaten cold slices of beef and biscuits Suzanne provided before he returned to his house and fallen asleep. This morning, he'd woken to a quiet house and a loneliness never experienced before Isaac entered his life. A moment later, his thoughts turned to May.

He'd seen another side of her in the clinic. May's worry over Clare, the despair on her face at the injuries the older woman suffered, demonstrated the deep compassion she held inside. The more he learned about the sweet, guileless young woman, the more Caleb craved her, became more determined to keep her in his life.

"Such a tragedy."

Caleb cringed at the patronizing voice of May's stepmother. Glancing at the amused looks on Beau's and Cash's faces, he turned to look at the woman.

"Yes, it is."

Pauline huffed. "If the church had been in a larger city, the fire department would've been able to save it."

Crossing his arms, Caleb tilted his head, his expression blank. "It's doubtful, Mrs. Bacon. I've read about fires destroying blocks of buildings in New York. The people of Splendor were able to contain the damage to the church. I believe any reasonable person would consider that a success."

Ignoring his comment, her lips twisted. "It's a pity a woman inside the church died." There wasn't a hint of remorse in her voice.

Steely eyes glared down at her, but he kept his voice neutral. "We didn't find any bodies, Mrs. Bacon."

Her eyes narrowed on him. "You must be mistaken," she huffed. "A deputy carried a body from the church. My son saw it."

"Mrs. Billings was found *outside* the church. She's recuperating at the clinic. If you'll excuse me, ma'am." Turning his back on her, Caleb glared at Beau and Cash, who worked to smother their laughter.

He shook his head, knowing he shouldn't let the unpleasant woman bother him. Then Caleb thought of the venom she directed at May, and at him. Anger at the callous way May's stepmother treated her grew each time he saw the woman. He had a hard time understanding how the congenial Dilly Bacon could live with such a vicious shrew, a woman so different from the man's daughter.

"Caleb!"

He whirled around, a smile tugging at his mouth when he spotted May on the steps of the St. James. Wiping his hands down his pants, he walked toward her.

"Good morning, May." His gaze raked over her, warmth constricting his chest. "You look lovely this morning."

Her face brightened at the compliment. "Thank you, Caleb." She could feel her face heat at his continued scrutiny.

Shifting in discomfort, Caleb cleared his throat, nodding at the hotel. "Are you going to work this early?"

"Lena sent a message to Suzanne about making extra meals for those working on the new church. Reverend Paige stayed up all night, going over plans with Bull Mason, Gabe, and Nick Barnett." She mentioned one of the foremen at Redemption's Edge, who also worked as a building designer, and Suzanne Barnett's husband. "Reverend Paige approved the drawing a few hours ago. Dax and Luke are sending men from the ranch to help."

Massaging his neck, he blew out a surprised breath. "They aren't wasting any time."

"Well, Christmas *is* only a couple weeks away. Everyone wants the church rebuilt by then."

Between Mack's wedding, learning about Isaac, calling on May, and the fire, he'd forgotten about the approaching holiday. Of course the town would want the church completed by Christmas Eve.

Caleb thought of his family in New York. The same as him, they'd been strong supporters of the North, even providing financial backing. They'd attended rallies, congratulating families whose sons had chosen to enlist.

That was why their reaction to hearing of his desire for a commission in the Union Army had been such a shock. His parents raged about the stupidity of fighting. He was a Covington, part of the business elite. No one expected him to put his life on the line when there were so many others willing to sacrifice themselves for the cause. Caleb and his father argued well into the night, shouting words they could never take back. Afterward, Caleb had stormed upstairs, stuffed belongings into a satchel, and left.

Although he'd written letters to them during the war, spoken of the battles and his commission to major, he'd never heard back. Not one word in all that time. Their silence told him all he needed about their true feelings for him. He hadn't returned, never spent another Christmas with his family.

Shoving aside the painful memory, Caleb stepped closer to May. "Will you spend Christmas with Isaac and me?"

Her mouth dropped open, eyes widening at the invitation. A brilliant smile appeared on her face as she reached out, placing a hand on his arm. "I'd love to celebrate with you and Isaac. As long as you let me cook."

Leaning down, he kissed her cheek. "I wouldn't have it any other way."

Chapter Eight

Redemption's Edge Ranch

Dax Pelletier pulled his coat collar up around his neck, warding off the chill from the dropping temperatures. They'd lost several head of cattle to wolves in the last month, and his patience had run out.

His brother, Luke, and a third of their men had ridden into Splendor that morning to help rebuild the church. Although it left the ranch shorthanded for a few days, it was the right decision.

"Could be we've got two packs killing the cattle, boss." Dirk Masters, one of the two foremen at Redemption's Edge, sat atop Banshee, scanning the tracks around them. "Tat found the remains of another steer a hundred yards north of here."

Dax blew out a crisp expletive. "Seems odd to have two active wolf packs so close together. We haven't been hit with the worst of the winter weather yet, and we've already lost more cattle than all of last year."

"Don't often see it. Fact is, I've never seen two packs so close. You've got to wonder what's going on. Strange, though. A couple of the steers weren't mauled like you'd expect if the wolves were killing for food."

Dax rubbed the stubble on his chin. "You're sure it's wolves?"

"The longer this goes on, the less sure I am. Even with the tracks, the remains have been so ravaged, it would've been hard to tell what brought them down. Tat and Johnny are spending time scouting the area around the last kill. Truth is I'm thinking we've got two things going on. A pack killing, and also foraging off the remains of other cattle killed by men."

"What about grizzlies?" Dax asked.

"When Travis took a look at the first two, he didn't see bear tracks." Dirk mentioned their best horse trainer and tracker, Travis Dixon, Isabella's husband. "Could be cougars. Travis took Isabella and Isaac, along with a wagonload of tools, into town this morning. When he gets back, we'll ride out and check the tracks again. I'm just hoping we don't find evidence of any wild-eyed, rabid critters."

Dax hoped they'd find anything but the crazed animals that killed out of rage rather than hunger. He'd heard of packs of rabid wolves prowling close to small towns in Wyoming and Idaho. It wouldn't be hard to believe the animals could appear in western Montana.

"There isn't much else we can do, other than track them. With half our men in town, including Travis, we don't have enough ranch hands to do more than guard the herd." Dax blew out a frustrated breath. "We just have to get them through winter and drive them to market."

Dirk shook his head, chuckling. "Then we'll do the same all over again next year. It's a good life, boss, knowing what's expected. I'm going to catch up with Tat and Johnny, ask them if they've found anything else."

Dax watched him ride out, shoving his hat down further on his head. His thoughts wandered to Savannah, Georgia. This time of year, his hometown would be rainy but warm. A lot warmer than western Montana.

Before the war, he'd captained one of his family's ships, hauling goods north. Luke would have been breeding and training thoroughbreds, and wooing the pretty women who flocked to him in droves.

That was before the destruction of Savannah by General Sherman during his March to the Sea. Their lives now didn't compare to what he and Luke had imagined their future to be when they were younger and much more idealistic.

Even so, neither would change anything. They'd built a good life in Splendor, made friends, married, and had children.

Their only regret might be the dangers of carving out a life in the vast, untamed frontier compared to the relative civility of the Eastern Seaboard. Wolves were just one of the threats, but there were many more.

An odd chill of unease ran down Dax's spine. He placed a hand on the butt of his rifle, scanning the area around him. Instincts had kept him alive during the war, and he continued to take them seriously.

"If you'd done exactly what I ordered, she'd be dead, not recuperating at the clinic."

He whirled around, crossing his arms. "It wasn't my fault she got out through the back door. It was locked. I never thought she'd have the strength to kick it open."

"How many times have I told you not to assume anything?"

"Quite often," he muttered, shoving his hands into his pockets.

"Well, all isn't lost. She didn't die, but she's weak and it will take time for her to recover. The older doctor isn't allowing anyone else to watch over her. At lunch, I overheard someone saying he'll be moving her to his house behind the clinic."

He nodded, understanding what this meant. "He'll have to sleep at some point."

"Exactly. If we can't get to her at his house, we'll be able to try again once she returns to the hotel. We cannot allow her to leave Splendor. Once she's gone, we'll never have to worry about anything again."

A wicked smile played at the corners of his mouth. "Don't worry."

"That's all I do when I must rely on you to do anything."

He jerked at the hard rebuke, knowing he should be used to them by now.

"You cannot muddle this up a second time. I doubt we'll get another chance."

His jaw clenched, face turning a mottled shade of red. "I won't allow her to leave alive," he ground out, hands fisted at his sides. "I *will* take care of this."

Whipping around, he stomped from the room, slammed the door, and bounded down the stairs.

Caleb worked next to Travis and a couple dozen men, clearing the debris in preparation for building the new church. Isabella's husband had assured him his wife would stay with Isaac as long as Caleb needed her. Still, it bothered him he hadn't had a minute to traverse the short distance to his home to see his son.

Not one of the men had stopped for lunch, taking the cold meats and fruit the women passed around, continuing their work as they ate. They'd given themselves five days to get the walls and roof up, another five days to complete the inside, paint the outside, and install new pews.

Unlike the old church, this one would have a belfry. Reverend Paige had already ordered the bell through Sylvia at the general store, but it wouldn't be delivered for weeks.

"You've got quite the little boy, Caleb."

He straightened at Luke's voice, unable to conceal the surge of pride. "I hope Isaac wasn't too much trouble."

"None at all. I think running around with the other children at the ranch was good for him. You remember Patrick, Dax's oldest son?"

Caleb nodded.

Luke chuckled. "Well, he loved having a boy around his own age to play with. Bull's son, Joshua, even tried to keep up. And Margaret and Mary loved playing big sisters to another boy."

The words rolled through Caleb, his mind working to make sense of them. He still had a hard time thinking of himself as a father, talking to other men about their children, and knowing how to respond. Pinching the bridge of his nose, Caleb looked up at Luke, doing his best to hide his befuddled expression.

Laughing at the look on his face, Luke clasped him on the shoulder. "Don't worry about it. Given enough time, being a father will make sense." Dropping his hand, his expression sobered. "I know it must be hard, having Isaac turn up without warning."

"Yeah. I had no idea Sadie was pregnant. She never said a word to me."

"So you *do* remember the girl." Luke's words weren't harsh, a statement of fact.

Caleb nodded. "She was a close friend of my fiancée, Regina." When Luke's brows rose, he winced. "She was murdered by some outlaws who rode through Austin.

After a while, when the whiskey stopped helping, I turned to Sadie." He shook his head, feeling another wave of guilt. "She's the one who helped me get through it all." Taking off his hat, he ran fingers through his hair. "Regina was from a prominent family. Sadie worked in a saloon. I always marveled at how the two could be such good friends. I didn't do right by Sadie and I'll always regret it." When Luke didn't respond, he shrugged. "Didn't mean to burden you with my problems." Turning to leave, he stopped when Luke put a hand on his shoulder.

"Maybe you could've done some things different, but it doesn't help to blame yourself. You've got a son to raise, and from what I've heard, a good woman to court. Hanging on to guilt won't do you any good, Caleb." Luke lowered his hand. "Trust me on this. We've all had to deal with mistakes and the guilt they cause. You've got to let it go."

Scrubbing a hand down his face, he nodded. "I tell myself the same every day."

Luke snorted out a knowing chuckle. "It'll get better in time."

"Hey, Luke. You got a minute?"

They looked toward the sound of Bull's voice. "Remember what I said." Luke dashed off, leaving Caleb to consider what he'd said. He figured it would be a long time before the guilt got any easier to bear.

"Caleb. Are you all right?"

May's worried voice broke through his internal struggle. Shifting to look at her, an odd peace washed over him. He didn't quite know what to think of the brief harmony May brought him. Shoving aside thoughts of Sadie, he walked toward her.

"I'm fine, May." Caleb wanted to draw her into his arms, use the warmth of her touch to comfort him. Now wasn't the time. "We've got a lot of work to do."

He glanced behind him, watching the way everyone scurried about, removing debris and raking the ground to get rid of the smaller fragments.

"Gabe says you'll be ready to start building the floor and walls tomorrow. Maybe install the roof a few days later." May clasped her hands together, biting her lower lip. "I should let you get back to work." Sliding her hands into the pockets of her coat, she turned to leave.

"May?"

Stopping, she looked over her shoulder at him. "Yes?"

"I don't know when I'll be able to see you."

Shifting to face him, she shrugged. "I understand. Everyone's working long hours. Probably won't be getting much sleep until the church is finished." She thought of his son. "Do you have someone to stay with Isaac?"

He nodded. "Isabella."

Of course, she thought, but wouldn't voice it. Isabella was a wonderful woman, someone Caleb could depend on to take care of Isaac.

"That's good. Well, I should be going."

He opened his mouth to stop her, then shut it. Caleb didn't miss the look of disappointment which crossed her face when he mentioned Isabella. He needed to get a few minutes alone with her, ask May what about Isabella bothered her so much.

Didn't she understand he needed someone he could depend on, a woman who'd taken care of children before, to watch over Isaac?

Then he remembered her conversation with Doc McCord. May had volunteered to watch over Clare Billings when she wasn't working. Offered to arrive at the clinic early each morning and stay until mid-afternoon when she had to leave for work.

He'd never really thought about what May did during the long hours of each day before going to the Eagle's Nest. Her closest friend, Sylvia, worked at the general store during the day. Since Isaac arrived, Gabe had Caleb working days. He used to make rounds at night, but no longer.

Recalling the way she and Isaac played together, her patient, easy manner, he smiled. No matter her amount of experience, May loved children, had a way with them. He'd watched her join the younger ones in their games after church. She'd even volunteered to start a children's class during the service, the same as many churches in the east offered.

"Hey, Caleb. You going to stand around the rest of the day?"

He looked up to see Mack watching him, a broad grin on his face. Deciding he needed to give the idea of May taking care of Isaac more thought, he walked toward his friend.

"Saw you talking to May. Is everything all right with you two?"

It was a good question. One he wasn't certain he could answer right now. Instead, he nodded. "Seems all right."

"Good. Gabe wants us to head to the jail and relieve Hex and Zeke. It'll give you a chance to check on Isaac." Mack got Gabe's attention, letting him know they'd be heading to the jail. "You may want to clean up while you're there."

Holding out his arms to look down at himself, he realized his shirt was covered in dirt and grime.

"Your face is worse." Mack jumped away when Caleb made to shove him. "Take your time. When you get back, I'll clean up and go talk to Sylvia a few minutes. Darn woman didn't come outside all day to say hello."

Caleb chuckled, his face sobering when he spotted May outside the boardinghouse. He had to blink a couple times before he recognized the man beside her.

"When did Dom Lucero get back in town?" Caleb liked Sylvia's brother. He'd been accepted into the Texas Rangers right before traveling to Splendor in search of his sister. When her relationship with Mack hit a rough spot, Dom had almost talked her into going back to Texas with him.

"This morning. He's staying at the St. James. After our wedding, he rode as far as Denver before deciding to turn back. I haven't had a chance to talk to him, but I'm pretty sure it has to do with a lady he met here."

"That so?" Caleb's body tensed, hands fisting at his sides when he saw the bright smile on May's face, then heard her laugh.

"Don't believe it's May, though." Mack's voice didn't sound as certain as Caleb would've liked. "Then again, she *is* a real pretty woman."

If Mack wasn't his closest friend, Caleb would've been tempted to land a blow to his jaw. When May reached out, placing a hand on Dom's arm, he was ready to stalk toward them, let the man know the way of it.

"Come on. We'd best relieve Hex and Zeke so you can see Isaac." When it took Caleb a moment to get moving, Mack slapped him on the back. "You can have a talk with Dom later. And if you want my opinion—"

"I don't."

Mack held up both hands, not worrying about the smile tugging at his lips.

"I can take care of any misunderstandings with May."

Opening the jail door, Mack lifted a brow. "Then I suggest you get to it."

Chapter Nine

"It is such a pleasure to meet you, Baron Klaussner." Words gushing out, Pauline made a slight curtsy.

"The pleasure is mine, madam." Ernst turned toward Dilly, extending his hand. "It's been a while."

Dilly grasped the offered hand. "Too long." He looked at his wife. "Ernst left Germany and moved to New York years ago. He's friends with Sheriff Evan's father, Walter." Dilly turned back to Ernst. "I'd heard you'd traveled west, but wasn't quite sure I believed it."

"At Walter's recommendation. Did you know he is here in Splendor, Dilly? He came to visit his son and decided to stay for a time. I've invited him and his family to join us for supper tonight."

"That's splendid, Ernst." Dilly's booming voice filled the parlor of the St. James. "I've not seen him in several years."

"Ah, there you are." Ernst moved around Dilly to greet Walter, Gabe and Lena Evans, and their son, Jackson.

After quick introductions, the group entered the Eagle's Nest. When all had been seated at a round table in a quiet alcove, Ernst ordered wine all around. After offering a toast, he looked at Dilly.

"What brings you to Splendor?"

"My daughter, May, moved here a year ago. I thought it was time to pay her a visit."

Lena's mouth curved into a grin. "May is one of our best employees." She ignored the sour expression on Pauline's face. "In fact, she has put forth an idea for adding pastries to our menu. I tasted her samples, and they are quite incredible."

Gabe reached over, settling a hand over his wife's. "I don't recall being invited to try her pastries."

"Nor I." Walter Evans lifted a brow before taking a sip of wine. "Perhaps we should ask May for a second tasting."

"I like pastries. May I try them?" At nine, Jackson occasionally showed the enthusiasm of a younger child.

Walter's lips twitched as he leaned toward Jackson. "Not if it means less for me, young man."

"But, Grandfather, I'm certain there will be enough. Isn't that right, Mother?"

Hiding her grin, Lena nodded. "Quite so, Jackson. I will speak with May tomorrow and ask for another tray of samples."

"May has always had a talent for cooking. She especially loves to bake. Takes after her dear mother in that respect." Dilly's comment was followed by an irritated hiss from the woman next to him. Pauline didn't like him speaking of his late wife. Most decidedly didn't appreciate him talking about her with such deep affection.

"I've heard your late wife often burnt pies and put too much flour in cakes." Pauline's mocking words echoed across the quiet table. She straightened her back, lifting her chin, satisfied with the barb until she noticed the disapproval on the faces of those around her. Shifting uncomfortably, her voice rang with disdain. "Well, it's what I've heard."

Embarrassed by her unfeeling words, Dilly sent her a scathing look. Leaning close, he lowered his voice in a critical tone. "I'm warning you. Do not humiliate me further."

Seeing her eyes widen in shock, he leaned away, a surge of satisfaction washing through him.

"I, too, would appreciate tasting May's pastries. Unfortunately, my wife has no interest and won't be attending." Dilly ignored her gasp, not sparing Pauline a glance.

Deflecting the obvious tension between Dilly and Pauline, Lena smiled. "Then it's settled. I'll go speak to May right now." She waited until the men stood and Gabe pulled out her chair. "I won't be gone long."

Waiting until she disappeared into the kitchen, Gabe picked up his glass of wine, looking at Dilly. "I understand you breed and train racehorses."

Eyes bright with pride, he nodded. "I've been breeding the best thoroughbreds in the eastern states for over twenty years. Many became champions, and even more are prized sires."

"Have you had a chance to visit the Pelletier ranch?" Gabe asked.

Interest piqued, Dilly shook his head. "Why, no. Do they raise thoroughbreds?"

Gabe shook his head. "The finest cattle horses this side of the Mississippi. They started with a few foundation sires they brought out from back east, crossing them with wild mustangs and a few domesticated horses raised by the Shoshone of southern Idaho." He chuckled. "Those were hard to obtain. Luke Pelletier spent a great amount of time and did a good deal of negotiating to acquire those horses."

"Fascinating," Dilly breathed out. "I would be quite appreciative if you'd provide an introduction to the Pelletiers."

"Have you seen the men working to rebuild the church?" Walter asked.

"Of course."

"Most of them are from the Pelletier ranch. I spoke to Luke yesterday. I'd be happy to introduce you tomorrow, Dilly."

"That would be splendid, Walter. Afterward, perhaps I can arrange to visit his ranch."

At the sound of footsteps, they turned to see Lena approach. After Gabe helped her into the chair, she leaned forward, resting her wrists against the edge of the table.

"May will have the samples ready tomorrow afternoon. Now, is everyone ready to eat?"

Ignoring the annoyed glances and spiteful comments from Gary, May assembled the items she needed to create her pastries for tomorrow. Lena had been clear. If the samples passed the tasting, they would be added to the menu and May would be the one preparing them.

Her body prickled with excitement. She'd started to believe Lena had forgotten her request to add pastries to the menu. When she'd entered the kitchen, making her request, May had been stunned. Now that her mind had cleared, she sorted through the possibilities of what she'd make.

"You still have work to do." Gary didn't look up as he ground out the words. Never easy to work with, he'd become unbearable since Lena gave the approval to add the items. May didn't doubt the tasting would go well.

"I'm almost finished." Her bright tone brought a scowl from Gary, but she was much too excited to care. She had a few items to clean and put away, then she could concentrate on what to fix for tomorrow.

May thought of Caleb, wondering if it would be too improper to stop by his house before going back to Suzanne's. She couldn't wait until tomorrow to tell him the news.

Finishing the last of her work, May hurriedly removed the apron and slipped on her coat. "I'll be in early tomorrow." She hurried from the kitchen through the side door, leaving no time for Gary to respond.

Stepping onto the boardwalk, May hesitated, biting her lower lip as she wrestled with the decision. The boardinghouse was less than two hundred feet away, Caleb's house a little farther. As she debated, May noticed a light snowfall began blanketing the ground. If it kept up, the town would be covered by morning.

Making a hasty decision, she raised the collar of her coat and hurried across the street. She slipped between two buildings, not stopping until she stood outside his front door. Brushing snow from her coat and bonnet, she noticed the lights on inside, but heard no sounds coming through the door. Sucking in a breath to calm her trembling, she lifted her hand and knocked. Not getting an answer, she raised her hand to try again, jumping back when the door drew open.

Caleb stood inside. He still wore his pants, but his shirt and boots were gone. She felt her mouth go dry at the sight.

Opening the door wide, he stepped outside and grabbed May's arm, pulling her inside. Shoving the door closed, his arms slipped around her before his mouth covered hers hungrily. Caleb meant to make it quick, but when her arms wrapped around his neck, he allowed the kiss to deepen. At the sound of her soft moan, he lifted his head and scooped May into his arms. Lowering himself onto the sofa, he settled her on his lap, reclaiming her mouth.

His lips gently caressed hers as his strong arms banded around her. Feeling her fingers dig into his arms,

Caleb groaned, aching need coursing through him. He let out a low growl when she squirmed against his lap, causing his body to harden. Knowing they had to stop, he raised his head, resting his forehead against hers.

Placing one last kiss on her temple, he drew away, looking into her glazed eyes. "I've been wanting to do that all day, sweetheart."

Trying to calm her pounding heart, she drew in a shaky breath. "You have?"

His lips lifted into a warm smile. "Sure have. It's been on my mind since I woke up this morning." Kissing her again, he settled her next to him, resting an arm around her shoulders. "Tell me what made you decide to visit me tonight?"

Swallowing to relieve the tightness in her throat, May blinked, trying to clear her head and remember why she had come to see him. Then her eyes widened.

"Oh, I have such wonderful news."

Caleb chuckled at the excitement in her voice. "Are you going to tell me what it is?"

Straightening, she turned toward him. "Lena asked me to bake more pastry samples for a tasting tomorrow. Gabe, Baron Klaussner, and my father will be there. If they like what I make, Lena will add them to the menu and *I'll* be in charge of baking them. Isn't it wonderful!" Her body buzzed with eager enthusiasm.

Chest tightening at the joy on her face, he cupped her face, brushing his mouth over hers. "It *is* wonderful news," he breathed against her lips before lifting his head. "Does it mean I'll get more samples, too?"

If possible, her face brightened even further. "You can have them anytime you want, Caleb." Scooting to the edge of the sofa, she stood. "I should be going. I have to be at the restaurant early tomorrow to make the pastries. If you want an early sample, come by the side door before noon." Smiling, she leaned down and kissed him.

Before he had a chance to stand, she'd rushed to the door and disappeared outside.

Charles sat in a chair next to Clare's bed, his hand protectively covering hers. It had been two days since the fire and she hadn't regained consciousness long enough to recognize him. Horrible, uncontrollable coughs wracked her entire body several times a day, then she'd fall asleep.

With Clay's help, he'd been able to get a few tablespoons of broth into her before she rolled to the side and coughed. At least she'd been able to keep most of the liquid down. This couldn't go on much longer, however. She'd continue to lose weight, lose strength, making it harder for her to recover, and Charles *needed* her to live.

Tomorrow would be the second day of rebuilding the church. Clay had kept him apprised of the men's progress while assuring Charles the clinic was fine without him for now.

Rosemary Masters, Dirk's wife, would continue to ride in from Redemption's Edge each day to help Clay. She'd been training for months with Rachel Pelletier, Charles's niece. Ever since Dax and Rachel had their second son, James, she'd been unable to provide regular nursing services at the clinic. Rosemary had been a blessing, especially with Charles tending to Clare.

Charles turned toward the window of the second bedroom in his home behind the clinic. Until now, he hadn't noticed the snow falling against the ink black darkness of the night. Pulling out his pocket watch, he checked the time. Almost ten o'clock.

He shifted back to the bed at the sound of Clare's ragged coughs. Lifting her head from the pile of pillows behind her, Charles gently rubbed her back.

"That's it, sweetheart. Expel the smoke from your lungs."

He and Clay had read everything in their journals about inhaling smoke during a fire. There'd been precious little to help with Clare's injury. Besides treatment recommendations for burns, they'd learned nothing.

Waiting through the coughing fit, he settled her back on the pillows before reaching for the glass of water. He lifted her head and touched it to her lips, encouraging her to drink.

"Come now, Clare. Try to drink a little."

His hand stilled when her eyes slowly opened. Holding his breath, he waited as she searched his face.

Blinking a few times, her lips parted, her eyes locking on his.

"I've been looking for you." The words came out on a raspy whisper before she began coughing again. When the episode ended, she met his gaze once more. "It is you, isn't it, Charles?"

Brushing hair from her face, he let his fingers trail down her cheek and along her jaw. "Yes, Clare. It's me."

Tears welled in her eyes, then spilled down her face. Charles brushed them away with his thumb.

"Don't cry, sweetheart." He felt moisture in his own, willing it away. Seeing the question in her eyes, he covered her hand with his. "You almost died in a fire. One of the deputies found you on the ground outside the church. Do you remember anything?"

She glanced away, staring out the window. "It's snowing."

A slight grin appeared on his face. "Yes. We get a good deal of snow in Montana. Much more than in Boston." He waited until she turned back to face him. "Do you recall the fire?"

Closing her eyes, Clare nodded. "I received a message to meet a friend in the church."

Brows furrowing, he gave her hand a light squeeze. "What friend?"

"Sylvia Mackey." She choked again. "How long have I been here?"

"Two days." He adjusted the pillows a little to help her. "The church and community building burned to the ground. The townsfolk have already begun rebuilding."

Her eyes widened. "Was anyone else..." Her voice trailed off, pain flashing across her face.

"No, sweetheart. You're the only one who was injured."

"What about Sylvia?"

"She's fine. She was inside the general store when the fire started."

Clare shook her head. "Are you certain?"

He nodded. "Yes, dear. Sylvia ran out of the store with several buckets and started helping with the fire."

She cleared her throat, wincing in pain. "But the note..."

Charles held the glass to her mouth, waiting until she'd taken several sips before answering. "You need to talk to the sheriff, Gabe Evans. My thought is Sylvia isn't the one who sent you the message."

Confused eyes met his. "Then who?"

Anger gripped him. Someone had tried to kill Clare. He'd let her go without a fight once. She'd given him a second chance, and Charles refused to fail her a second time.

"I don't know, but we're going to find out."

Chapter Ten

Caleb, Hex, Zeke, and several of the Pelletier men worked together to finish framing the walls. Due to several inches of snow, their progress had been slow. It had taken a while to shovel down to the work completed the day before. By eleven thirty, they'd made up for the time lost earlier in the morning. Caleb set down his hammer, stomach grumbling.

"I'm going to get something to eat. I'll meet you back here."

Hex brushed both hands down his coat. "You're welcome to join us at the boardinghouse."

A slow smile spread across Caleb's face. "Thanks, but I can't."

Careful not to step on any of the newly completed work, he headed between the St. James and the building next door. Knocking on the kitchen's side door, he hesitated a moment when May answered, beckoning him inside.

"Hurry. The chef is running errands and won't be back for a while." She dashed to one of the counters. Sweeping a cloth off a tray, May smiled. "There are a dozen pastries, plus roast beef and potatoes. Here." She grabbed a stool, setting it beside him. Turning away again, she selected flatware and two plates.

"Have you eaten?"

Picking up another stool, she set it next to his. "I thought we might share."

They split the food on the two plates, Caleb taking large bites while May picked at hers. She'd sent a guarded look at him every few minutes, a fierce longing tugging at her. May didn't notice when Caleb set down his utensils.

"Are you all right, May?"

Sucking in a breath at the concern on his face, she pushed the plate away. May didn't want to ruin another meal with him. Still, she had no desire to continue with their courtship without understanding what bothered him so much about his past.

"I'm just wondering why you've never taken the time to tell me of your past." Reaching over, she placed a hand on his arm. "And you aren't allowed to walk out on me again."

Pinching the bridge of his nose, he blew out a weary breath. The lighthearted nature of their meal lost, he met her expectant gaze.

"There hasn't been much time, May. I'm not avoiding it."

She lifted a brow. "No?"

"You deserve to hear everything, ask questions, and make a decision about continuing to see me."

"When, Caleb?"

"With Isaac, rebuilding the church, and my job, I don't know when there'll be enough time. Perhaps after Christmas."

"Christmas." She whispered the word too low for him to hear. Ignoring the ache in her heart, May lifted her hand from his arm, slipping off the stool. She glanced at his empty plate. "Are you finished?"

Studying her solemn features, he nodded, watching as she covered the tray with the cloth. Picking it up, she held it out to him.

Hesitating an instant, he took it. "I should be going. I'll need to get this home before returning to help with the construction."

She nodded. "All right."

"I hope the tasting goes well, May. You deserve to have something wonderful happen to you."

Squaring her shoulders, she nodded. "Yes, I do."

Walking to the door, she held it open, heart thudding when he left, making no mention about seeing her again. The realization he had no intention of sharing his past hit her as hard as a blow to the stomach.

He'd had plenty of time when they rode out of town before the fire. Although she loved the way he kissed her breathless last night, he could've spent the time explaining what was so awful she wouldn't want to see him. Even today, he could've been the one to bring it up, let her know he *did* intend to talk to her.

She didn't blame him for avoiding the discussion. Caleb had too many responsibilities already. He shouldn't feel obligated to call on her, knowing he'd need to share the past if they were to continue seeing each other. She wanted to make his life easier, not more difficult.

May swallowed the truth, a sharp pain ripping through her as she accepted what had to be done. He was too honorable to call it off. As much as it hurt, May would have to be the one to set him free.

Perhaps in time, when his life settled into a comfortable routine, he might seek her out, request to start seeing her again. Right now, he didn't deserve another obligation, and that was all she was. May didn't doubt he liked her, cherished their friendship, but she wanted more. She deserved more. She deserved love.

Swiping away the tears beginning to slip down her face, she lifted a hand, pressing it against her heart. There was no reason to have the conversation today or even tomorrow. Caleb had already told her he didn't have time to talk until maybe after Christmas, and May believed Lena would approve the pastries, requiring more hours at the Eagle's Nest.

She snorted. Perhaps there wasn't a reason to have a discussion at all. The courtship May believed held so much promise would fade, both of them going on as before.

May hoped they'd find a way to keep their friendship. She wouldn't allow herself to expect anything more.

"Do you feel well enough to get out of bed for a few minutes, Clare?" Charles held out a bathrobe, a hopeful grin on his face.

She'd been awake since early morning, ate a decent lunch, making comments about going back to her room at the St. James. Charles had no intention of letting her get that far away from him ever again.

Over the long hours sitting by her bed, he allowed himself to recall the painful memories he usually shoved aside. When he did think of Clare, it generally came late at night with a bottle of whiskey.

They'd been young, believing love would solve any problems they'd face. How naïve of them. He'd been from a prominent Boston family. Clare's father, brother, and most male relatives worked the docks, making a decent, albeit difficult, living. When his father learned of the love between Charles and Clare, he'd made her father a financial proposition.

Still, the two promised their future to each other. He left for medical school, assured she'd wait for him. A few months later, he'd received word Clare had married a man of her father's choosing and left Boston. Although he'd never seen her again, Charles prayed she'd found happiness with a good man, someone who would treat her well, giving Clare the family she'd always wanted. Staring at her as she sat on the bed, he wondered how much of what he hoped had come true.

"I'd love to get out of bed for a while, Charles. Maybe I could sit in your living room." She glanced up at him. "Assuming you have one."

Charles chuckled at what she must think of his small home. "Yes, I do. I even have a kitchen and another bedroom where I sleep. Everything I need." *Except you.*

Helping her from the bed, he held the robe while she slid into it, then tied the belt. Charles wrapped an arm around her waist, leading her into the short hall.

"This is my room," he nodded toward a door. "The living room is through here. It's been snowing, so I keep a fire burning in all four stoves. The kitchen and dining area are through there." He motioned to a door across the room.

Clare's gaze took in everything, wide eyes looking up at him. "It's lovely, Charles."

A mirthless chuckle left his lips. "I'm sure it's nothing as nice as what you've become used to." He shrugged, refusing to apologize for his choices. Leading her to the sofa, he helped her down, taking a seat beside her.

"I left Boston not long after finishing medical school. For a time, I worked in a Chicago hospital, then moved to one in Philadelphia. After a while, I decided to travel west. Stories of the wild frontier always fascinated me. Not long before the war started, I got on a train, riding to the end of the line, then found passage in one of the many wagon trains heading west. I eventually reached Splendor and stayed."

Clare remained silent as Charles told her of his life after they'd been forced apart, feeling another tear to her heart. Throat clogging with emotion, all she could do was nod.

"It was best your father found a man more worthy of you, Clare. He did take care of you, didn't he?"

Clasping her hands in her lap, she stared at them, swallowing a painful ball of regret. It had taken all of a few seconds after seeing Charles's dear face to confirm her continued love for him. She'd never felt the same for her husband, a man her father thought had been so perfect for her.

"We moved to Chicago immediately after the wedding. I wished I'd known you worked at the hospital. Maybe we could've found a way..." Her voice faded on the ridiculous thought.

Placing a hand over hers, Charles shook his head. "We can't go back, Clare. Tell me more about your life."

Biting her lip, she nodded. "My husband worked hard, provided a good home, although he was absent most of the time. He made good money. I suspected most of it was illegal." She glanced at him before switching her attention out the window. "We never had children. I did hear he had several with the mistress he kept. Apparently, he'd been with her long before we married. I never understood why he accepted my father's offer to marry me when he loved another woman."

She looked back at him. "I learned my father *and* yours offered him an extraordinary amount of money to take me out of Boston and never return. It could only be done through a legal marriage. When he died of heart failure, it was a blessing." A humorless smile tipped the corners of her mouth. "His entire estate came to me, including several houses. I sold all but the one where his mistress lived, provided a monthly allowance for her, and packed my belongings." Her eyes sparkled. "For the first time in my life, I felt an incredible sense of freedom. I could've gone anywhere, but I knew there was just one person I wanted to find."

Charles looked at her, an interesting thought crossing his mind. "You hired someone to find me."

She nodded. "Allan Pinkerton's agency. Seems he already had a file on several people in Splendor, some who had been agents for him. It took less than two weeks to confirm your location. I left right away."

The hopeful look on her face had his chest constricting. Settling an arm over her shoulders, he drew Clare to him, placing a kiss on her forehead. "This is exactly where you should be, sweetheart."

A sob broke free before she could stop it. "Do you think..." She sobbed harder, swiping at tears.

Gaze warming, the corners of his mouth slid into a tender smile. "As soon as you're healed, we'll marry. That is, if you still love me and can live with a humble frontier doctor in his modest home."

Lips parting, trying to control her sobs, she nodded, hiccupping her response. "Yes, Charles. Definitely, yes."

"I heard from Doctor McCord that Clare is doing better. He expects Doctor Worthington to return to the clinic soon."

"Which means she'll be alone," he replied, a feral grin appearing. "Is she going back to the St. James?"

"I don't know. It won't matter. As long as she's not being watched, we'll be able to get to her. We just have to pick the right time."

"And the right method," he responded. "We cannot try to hide her death with another fire."

"No. We'll need to come up with another way. And you *cannot* fail this time."

His features hardened, nostrils flaring at the rebuke. He nodded, anger at the person a few feet away stopping him from saying or doing what he wanted. An idea formed as he watched the calculating look on the other's face.

If their plan worked, he saw no reason to share the money passing to him after Clare's death. Chuckling to himself, he began to rethink his future, coming up with a very satisfying solution.

Leaning down, Caleb lifted one corner of the church wall while several other men lifted the rest. In less than thirty minutes, the last of four walls was up and secured in place.

"That's it today, men." Bull's loud voice boomed across the site. The Pelletier men would head to the ranch, returning in the morning. The others, mainly townsfolk, would go home, showing up at sunrise to start another day of building.

Caleb let out a satisfied sigh. Even with the snow, they'd made incredible progress. If they kept up this pace, the church would be finished and ready for Christmas service.

"I'll go back to the jail and see if Gabe wants anyone else besides Hex and Dutch to keep watch tonight. If so, I'll take it while you take care of Isaac." Mack scrubbed a hand down his face, looking over his shoulder at the skeleton of the church. "It's going to be real nice when we finish. Sylvia said she, May, and a few other women are already planning for decorations."

"Of course they are." He thought of May, the way he'd taken the extra food and left earlier. Every time she mentioned wanting to hear of his past, he closed up, which didn't make sense since he'd been the one to tell her she needed to hear about the things he'd done, all his regrets.

The more time they spent together, the more certain he was of his desire to marry May and have more children. Caleb didn't want to admit the truth, didn't

120

want her to hear about his life and walk away. After seeing her today, he became less certain of his ability to keep the story from her. Something in her manner when he left the restaurant worried him.

He'd thought about their conversation. All seemed fine until he mentioned not having much time to talk until after Christmas. A little over a week away, yet to some people, it might feel like forever. Caleb wondered if his comment had been what caused the distress on May's lovely face.

Rubbing the back of his neck, he mumbled a curse. If his reluctance to talk had been what caused the change, he needed to do something about it, and before Christmas. He wanted May, couldn't imagine seeing her with another man. The blue-eyed beauty was meant for him and Isaac, no one else.

Casting a look at the St. James, he considered returning to the side door, requesting a time when they could meet and talk. Glancing at the darkening sky, he decided it could wait another day. He had a son waiting for him, and Isabella needed to get home to prepare supper for Travis. Like the other men, Travis had been working long hours on the church. He deserved to be with his wife.

"How are you and May doing?"

Caleb jerked, forgetting Mack still stood by his side. "Fine," he lied.

Regardless of what had happened on his sofa the night before, instinct told him May didn't cherish it as much as she wanted the truth of his past.

"Sylvia wants to have you, May, and Isaac over for supper sometime. She'd like it to be before Christmas, and I try to give her whatever she wants." Mack shrugged, a smile tugging at his lips.

"It's not so simple with May working nights. Maybe this Sunday after church would be all right with her. She has to report to the restaurant by three o'clock."

Mack's brows furrowed. "Is Reverend Paige planning to still have a service? The church won't be close to ready by Sunday."

Caleb chuckled. "Nick Barnett said he could use the Dixie. We'll see how many people attend church inside a saloon. I'm certain most of the women have never seen the inside of one."

"You might be surprised. Women are curious, the same as the rest of us. I'd wager a good number will attend just to see where their men drink and play cards." Mack left the rest of the saloon's activities unsaid.

"I'll talk to May. I'm sure she'll want to be there." At least he knew she'd want to have supper with Sylvia and Mack.

After explaining his past, Caleb hoped she would still choose to be with him and Isaac.

Chapter Eleven

May hadn't been able to wipe the smile from her face since Lena gave her the good news. Her pastries would be added to the menu Wednesdays, Fridays, and Saturdays to start. If they sold well, Lena and the other partners would decide about adding them on other days.

Before leaving the kitchen, Lena gave her another piece of good news. May's hours would change. She'd work from early morning to late afternoon on the days pastries were offered. On Thursdays, she'd do her regular kitchen duties from mid-afternoon until the restaurant closed. She'd be off Sundays, Mondays, and Tuesdays, free to do whatever she wanted.

Her enthusiasm faded when she thought of telling Caleb the good news. Even with her decision to end the courtship, allowing him to focus on Isaac and his job, he was still the first person she thought of seeing after Lena gave her the decision.

Lena had told her to clean up and go home early. Gary hadn't been thrilled, but said nothing after learning they'd be hiring someone to take May's place on the days she didn't work or left early.

Removing her apron, she slipped into her coat. "Good night," she called before heading out the back door, ignoring Gary's whispered mutterings.

Dashing across the main road, she headed to the next street where Sylvia and Mack lived beside Caleb and

Isaac. Emerging between two buildings, she glanced between the two houses, pursing her lips.

Sylvia would be thrilled for her. So would Caleb, and she'd get to see Isaac. It was early enough the boy would still be awake. She didn't want to interrupt their supper or the quiet time they spent together.

Sighing, she started toward Sylvia's house, stopping when Caleb's door opened, Isaac running outside. Stepping into the shadows, she watched the little boy jump down the steps to launch himself into a pile of freshly fallen snow. Giggles tightened her throat as deep masculine laughter caught her attention.

Caleb stood on the small porch, hands in his pockets as he watched his son toss snow everywhere. He hadn't seen May on the other side of the narrow street. She took the time to watch father and son talk as Isaac played, joy on both their faces.

"May!"

She jerked at her name coming from Isaac. Seeing the look of surprise on Caleb's face, she stepped from the shadows. A smile lit her face.

"Hello, Isaac." Swallowing, she shifted her gaze. "Caleb."

Taking the steps to the street, Caleb stood in front of her, searching her face. "What are you doing here, May?" He must've seen the flash of pain. Cupping her face in both hands, he leaned down, brushing a kiss across her lips. "It doesn't matter. I'm just glad to see you. Come on. Let's go inside." He put an arm over her shoulders, guiding her up the steps, stopping at the door. "Time to get into the house, Isaac."

After some grumbling, his son stomped up the steps. Waiting as Caleb brushed the snow from his clothes, Isaac bounded inside, shrugging out of his coat and mittens before hurrying to his box of toys.

"The box is almost full." May walked toward where Isaac sat on the floor, taking out several toys.

"The Pelletiers brought some. Suzanne and Nick also contributed, as did Lena and Gabe. I'm warming up stew. Can you stay and have supper with us?"

Her body relaxed at the invitation. She should return to the boardinghouse, have supper alone, then go to bed.

"I'd love to stay." Placing her coat on a hook by the door, she joined Caleb in the kitchen. "How can I help?"

"We're just having stew and biscuits. You could get the plates and flatware."

She didn't have to ask where he kept them. After setting the table, she walked over to kneel next to Isaac. "What are you building?"

He didn't look up. "A church."

She shot a look at Caleb, meeting his interested gaze.

"Papa building church."

"Yes, he is. And he's doing a very good job. It's going to be beautiful." She brushed a strand of hair from Isaac's forehead. "Yours is also going to be beautiful."

He nodded, continuing to focus on the blocks.

"Supper is ready." Caleb set the pot on the table, along with a bowl filled with biscuits.

May stood, holding out her hand to Isaac. "Time to eat."

Dropping the block, he stood, grasping May's hand. It only took a few steps to get to the table. Taking seats, they bowed their heads while Caleb said a prayer, Isaac whispering the words. He truly was a miniature of his father.

Caleb filled each plate, adding a biscuit before handing one to May and another to Isaac. Grabbing a plate for himself, he scooped up a large helping of stew. After a minute, he looked at May.

"How did the tasting go?"

She grinned, setting her fork down. "It went very well. In fact, much better than I hoped."

"Tell me."

She explained what happened, finishing with her changed hours. "So I'll work Wednesdays, Fridays, and Saturdays until late afternoon, then my regular hours on Thursdays."

His eyes widened. "So you won't be working Sundays, Mondays, and Tuesdays?"

"Yes. Isn't it wonderful?"

As May spoke, Caleb watched the joy on her face, the way her body thrummed at the opportunity, his heart squeezing. She had a talent, and now she had the chance to use it. He couldn't be more proud of her.

"Yes, May, it's wonderful news. You're quite talented. I'm very happy for you." Warmth spread through him at seeing her eyes sparkle at his compliment.

"They'll be on the menu this Friday, so I'll need to arrive extra early. I want everything to be perfect."

"I'm sure they will be, sweetheart." Finishing his meal, he glanced at Isaac's empty plate. "Would you like some more, son?"

Isaac nodded, lifting his plate. Caleb put a small amount in the middle, placing one more biscuit beside the stew. Setting down the spoon, he sat back, his gaze moving to May.

"I'll be putting Isaac to bed after supper. Do you have time to stay?"

She shifted in her seat. "I probably should—"

"I want to tell you about my past," he interrupted, his eyes filled with worry.

Lips parting, her brows lifted. "All right."

He relaxed, knowing the sense of peace wouldn't last long. Once she heard his story, there was an excellent chance she'd leave and their time together would be over.

May couldn't calm the unease knotting inside her. Back rigid, hands clasped in her lap, she sat on the edge of the sofa, waiting as Caleb paced back and forth. She didn't know how long she sat there before he spoke.

"My father and I didn't agree on my decision to fight for the Union." Caleb told her how he'd left the family home after a horrible argument with his father and joined the Union, fighting in more battles than he could remember. He told of the letters he'd sent, never receiving a reply.

Caleb admitted the lack of correspondence from his family was what made him decide to ride west to Austin, becoming a Texas Ranger. Stopping his pacing, he looked at May.

"That's where I met Regina."

May's face scrunched into a frown. "Regina?"

"My fiancée."

A gasp broke through May's lips. Sitting on a chair beside the sofa, Caleb massaged the back of his neck.

"Like you, Regina was beautiful and full of life. Her family was one of the wealthiest in Austin, yet she made friends with everyone. I don't believe anyone was a stranger to Regina. She loved everyone, and they loved her."

"And *you* loved her."

"Yes, May. I loved Regina very much."

She did her best to shove aside the ache at his admission. "What happened?"

Closing his eyes, images of that night came back as clear as if it had happened yesterday. Sucking in a shaky breath, he gazed across the room. "She got caught in the cross fire between three brothers and a couple other men."

May placed a hand over her mouth. The pain on his face shot to her heart.

"By the time I got to her, she was gone. One minute Regina was running toward me, her eyes glistening in excitement, as if she couldn't wait to tell me something. The next, she was dead." His voice broke on the last.

"I'm so very sorry, Caleb. I can't imagine what you went through after losing her."

Scrubbing a hand down his face, Caleb shook his head. "I didn't handle her death well. For a while, I took the most dangerous assignments, tracking the worst killers. My captain told me he thought I had a death wish." He lifted a shoulder. "Maybe he was right. Life didn't hold any meaning for me anymore."

Standing, he went to the kitchen and grabbed a bottle of whiskey. Pouring a glass, he tossed it back, letting the amber liquid burn down his throat. Setting down the glass, he walked back toward May, sitting on the chair. Leaning forward, he rested his arms on his legs, staring at the floor.

"Regina's good friend was a saloon girl. They were as close as sisters. The rich rancher's daughter and a young woman with no family."

"Sadie," she whispered.

With a quick glance up, Caleb nodded, returning his gaze to the floor. "I drank a lot, but couldn't kill the pain. One night, Sadie joined me at the bar. She missed Regina almost as much as I did. I don't recall how it happened, but I ended up in her bed. It was the first good sleep I'd gotten since Regina's death. After that, I returned at least once a week. We never spoke of love. Each of us needed something, and we were able to find it in bed." He looked up in time to see her wince. "If this is too difficult, I won't say more."

Taking a few slow breaths, she shook her head. "No. I want to hear it all."

"All right." He stood, walking to the window, staring out at the black night. "I don't know how long Sadie and I went on like that. Maybe a year. She helped me through the grief, and I hope I helped her. I'd planned to stay in Austin, try to build a life. One day, I saw wanted posters on the men who'd killed Regina. My captain refused to give me the assignment to hunt them down."

Turning back to her, he leaned against the wall, crossing his arms. "I became a bounty hunter, leaving Austin without telling Sadie goodbye. Not even a damn goodbye," he grated out, his voice full of self-loathing. Caleb shook his head, as if still trying to understand how he could've left the woman who'd helped him through the worst time of his life.

"I tracked down and killed two of them." Dropping his arms, he ran a hand through his hair. "I didn't give them a chance, May. The two were in a saloon, playing cards. I walked in, got their attention, and shot them. They were cold-blooded killings and I've never felt the slightest remorse. I stayed long enough to clear the deaths with the local sheriff, then rode out. For months, I tracked the third man, the one whose bullet killed Regina. I never found him."

Blowing out a breath, he pushed away from the wall. "I tracked him to South Pass City in Wyoming, then lost the trail. Instead of riding back to Austin, I rode north. Another decision I'll always regret."

Her face a mask, May nodded. "Because then you would've learned about Sadie being pregnant."

"Yes," he ground out.

Sitting down again, he sighed. "Mack and I served under Gabe during the war. I learned he'd gone to Splendor and decided to see what it was like. My money had run out and I needed work. Gabe hired me." His tortured eyes met hers. "You know the rest."

Pulling her gaze from his, she stared straight ahead, throat so tight she couldn't speak. He'd been through so much. Being shunned by his own family, the death of his fiancée, killing two men without a hint of remorse, and leaving Sadie behind. The woman who'd cared for him, helped him heal after Regina's death, had no way of finding him. He'd left her alone with no one to turn to. Her brows drew together.

"How did the woman who brought Isaac learn you lived in Splendor?"

"My captain. I let him know where I ended up. He paid the woman to escort Isaac to me. The man had always been good to me."

131

"So had Sadie." The words came out without thought. She wanted to take them back, yet couldn't. They were the truth.

Misery contorted his face. "Yes, she did. And I left her alone, with no one to depend on. I never even sent her one damn telegram." Pinching the bridge of his nose, he looked at her. "What kind of man does that to a woman who'd been nothing but kind and giving?"

Pushing up from the chair, he faced her. "Now you know why I'm not suitable for a fine woman like you, May."

Tearing her gaze from his, she rubbed her forehead, trying to make sense of all she'd learned. "I don't know what to think right now, Caleb. You've been through so much."

"And I've made a mess of most everything."

"No. You did what you thought was right at the time. It's always easy to look back and criticize our past actions."

"I hurt people I loved."

His scornful tone ignited May's anger. She stood, stepping next to him.

"We *all* hurt people we love."

"You don't. Regina didn't, and neither did Sadie."

Eyes widening, she took in his meaning. "Sadie loved you?"

Jaw tightening, he nodded. "Yes."

She couldn't move, could hardly breathe. "Did you love her?"

Drawing in a ragged breath, he shook his head. "I couldn't. Not after Regina."

"I see." But she didn't.

The woman who bore him a son loved Caleb, yet he'd left Sadie behind without a backward glance. Granted, he knew nothing of Isaac. Still, she'd professed to loving him, brought him back to life after Regina's death. Even if he couldn't return her love, didn't she mean enough for him to spare a few minutes for a farewell? May swallowed the pain she felt at the young woman's plight.

Placing a hand on her chest, she pressed, hoping to ease the ache.

Caleb watched the play of emotions on May's face, feeling like the worst kind of scoundrel.

"I should go." She didn't look at him as she slipped into her coat and bonnet. "Thank you for supper."

Stepping in front of her, he placed his hands on her shoulders. "I'll understand if you want to call off the courtship. I wouldn't hold any hard feelings toward you."

She lifted her face, staring into eyes full of misery and pain. "I don't know what I want right now, Caleb. There is much I have to think about. Can you allow me time to consider all I've learned?"

A slight rush of relief washed over him. "As much time as you need, May." He leaned down, placing a chaste kiss on her cheek. "May I still accompany you to church on Sunday?"

She thought a moment, slowly shaking her head. "I'm sorry, but I just don't know."

He gave a curt nod. "I understand." Standing aside, he opened the door. "No matter your decision, I hope we can remain friends."

So do I, she thought, but the words stuck in her throat. "Good night, Caleb."

Watching her hurry into the night, he let out a defeated breath. A pain he hadn't felt since losing Regina slashed through his chest, stalling his breath. Closing the door, he leaned against it, confusion crowding his thoughts.

He had so many regrets, and there wasn't one he could fix. Entering his room, Caleb lowered himself onto the bed. Until tonight, he didn't realize the full depth of his feelings for May, how much he cared about her, needed her in his life.

Falling back on the bed, he closed his eyes. Images of his parents, Regina lying dead in his arms, Sadie opening her heart to him, and the men he'd killed flashed across his mind.

Right now, though, the one haunting him most was the disillusionment and pain in May's eyes as she rushed out the door.

Chapter Twelve

"Are you sure you don't want to ride out to the Pelletier ranch with May and me?" Dilly picked up his hat, settling it on his head. "I'm told they breed the best horse stock in all of Montana."

Pauline's nose scrunched. "Maybe another time, dear. I thought to visit the millinery and general store today."

Dilly didn't argue. He still hadn't forgiven her for the offensive comments about his deceased wife. This trip had shown him another side of Pauline, and he didn't like what he'd seen or heard from her.

When they'd met, he hadn't felt a whit of attraction to the widow. Pauline had been persistent, showing up at social events he attended, inviting him to accompany her to various parties and soirees. She'd been attentive, almost fawning in her efforts to win him. Over time, he'd weakened, marrying the woman more for companionship than any real affection.

Her courteous manner had deteriorated on the trip west and hadn't improved since arriving in Splendor. The unexpected outburst in front of his friends at the Eagle's Nest had stunned him, and the sour feeling in the pit of his stomach hadn't eased.

"May and I will be gone most of the day. Should I invite Oliver?"

"I'd prefer he stay in town with me, Dilly. Besides, you know he doesn't care at all for horses."

Yes, he did know of his stepson's aversion to anything with four legs. He'd been raised a city dandy, and no matter how Dilly tried to open his mind to other activities, Oliver refused his efforts.

"Fine. Well, I'm off to meet May." He shot her a cursory glance before leaving their room. Reaching the lobby, a broad grin spread across his face. Walter and Ernst stood near the door.

"If you don't mind, we'll be riding along with you." Ernst slapped his riding gloves against his thighs. "It's been too long since I've been to the Pelletier ranch."

Dilly shook both their hands. "It's a grand idea. May will also be coming."

"Wonderful." Walter stepped outside, waiting until the other two joined him before the three walked down the steps. "They're making good progress with the church."

Over the last few days, the walls and roof had been completed, a few of the windows installed. The other openings would be covered until more windows arrived from Big Pine.

Dilly chuckled. "Yes, they are. I do have to say, it was a different experience having the service at the Dixie yesterday. I quite enjoyed it."

"My guess is you enjoyed the scenery upstairs as opposed to Reverend Paige's message." Walter referred to the saloon ladies who'd lined the upstairs railing, listening to the sermon.

Dilly cleared his throat. "They were a nice distraction."

The three continued down the boardwalk toward Noah's livery. May stood outside, tugging her coat around her.

The snow had stopped Saturday, giving the town a welcome reprieve. It wouldn't be an easy ride, but it wouldn't be as difficult as they'd expected.

"Here's your horse and your father's." Noah handed May two sets of reins. "I'll get the other two."

"Good morning, May." Dilly's voice boomed across the open expanse in front of the livery. Opening his arms, he encircled her in a tight embrace. "I'm glad you decided to come with us."

May nodded against his chest, shooting a furtive glance toward the jail before stepping away. She hadn't spoken to Caleb since the night he'd confessed his past, and she missed him terribly.

At church yesterday, he and Isaac had sat with Isabella and Travis on one side, Gabe's sister, Nora, and her husband, Wyatt Jackson, on the other. May had taken a seat across the room with Sylvia, Mack, and Sylvia's brother, Dom Lucero. When church ended, she'd walked out on Dom's arm, scanning the boardwalk and street, but hadn't found Caleb. Her heart still ached at the pain she'd seen on his face when she left his house the previous week.

"Thank you for inviting me."

She greeted Walter and Ernst, then mounted, reining the horse north, waiting for the others. Glancing over her shoulder once more, not spotting the one person she most wanted to see, she kicked the horse and rode out of town.

Caleb stood at the jail window, ignoring the pain in his chest at the sight of May riding away. He'd seen her look his way, not seeing him standing inside, and wondered if she felt the same loss as him.

He'd hoped to talk with May after church, but Isaac complained of a stomach ache. They'd barely made it home before his son lost his entire breakfast, then fell asleep. Caleb hadn't left his side all day or that night. Monday morning, Isaac woke ready to eat and play, as if he'd never been sick.

Caleb hesitated to leave after Isabella arrived to watch Isaac, acquiescing when she'd shooed him outside. An hour later, he stood at the jail window, sipping coffee. He'd been watching the men working to finish the church until a figure across the street caught his attention. May hurried across the street toward Noah's. Not long afterward, she'd ridden toward the Pelletier ranch with her father, Walter, and Ernst.

"What's going on with you and May?" Mack sat in one of the well-worn wooden chairs, holding a dented tin cup filled with coffee.

Making a slow turn toward him, Caleb's eyes narrowed. "What do you mean?"

Mack leaned back in the chair, his lips twisting with suspicion. "When was the last time you and May didn't sit together at church?"

His expression didn't change. "A while. Does Dom have an interest in her?" He hadn't meant to ask, grimacing when it was too late to take the question back.

"No, Dom doesn't have an interest in May, and don't change the subject. She won't say anything to Sylvia or me, so I'm asking you."

Shredding fingers through his hair, he blew out a disgusted breath. "I told her about my past."

Mack's brows lifted. "I'll be damned. I didn't think you'd ever share what you'd been through with anyone."

"Except you."

Mack gave a curt nod. "Except me." He blew across the top of his cup, taking a sip of the hot brew. "Did you tell her everything?"

Caleb nodded. "All of it."

Setting the cup down, Mack leaned forward, resting his arms on his legs. "What did she say?"

Frustration clouded his features. "Nothing. Not one damn word before she walked out." Scrubbing a hand down his face, Caleb lowered himself into a chair beside Mack. "She hasn't spoken to me since."

"We both know I'm not good at this, but it seems you might want to go to her. May's shy and tends to think too much. You may want to let her know you're still interested in seeing her. Do whatever's needed to get her to talk to you." A smirk crossed Mack's face. "Unless you no longer have an interest in her."

Caleb replied with a disgusted snort. "I plan to marry her. That's why it was so important she know about my past. It wouldn't be right to have her learn about it later."

Mack whistled. "Marry? I didn't know you'd made a decision."

"It doesn't do me much good if May can't understand why I made the decisions I did."

Scraping the chair over the wooden floor, Mack stood. "Do you want me to talk to Sylvia? Maybe she can get through to May, convince her to see you."

Caleb shook his head. "Thanks, Mack, but I need to be the one to approach May."

"She doesn't work today. Bring Isaac to our place this evening, then go find her." Mack clasped Caleb on the shoulder.

"What if she won't see me?"

Shaking his head, Mack chuckled. "Never thought I'd see a time when Caleb Covington could be cowered by a little bit of a woman."

Muttering several curses, Caleb stood. Grabbing his hat, he headed to the door. "I'll bring Isaac over after supper. You'd better let Sylvia know."

Slamming the door behind him, he headed up the boardwalk, his gaze landing on the men working on the church. Leaning against a post, Caleb watched. He'd rather be cutting boards or hammering nails. Something physical to take his mind off May.

"Hey, Caleb. Gabe allowing you to be a deputy today?" Dom Lucero brushed dirty hands down his coat, stepping onto the boardwalk next to him.

"Someone has to protect the town. I didn't know you'd decided to come back until Mack told me." Caleb studied Sylvia's brother, a Texas Ranger who'd come to Splendor in search of his sister. She'd run away from her wealthy family in Texas, arriving in town as a mail order bride with May and two other young women.

"I got as far as Denver and got a telegram from my captain. There's a man wanted for murder in Texas and is reported to be in Montana. I turned around and came back." Dom looked up at the clear sky. "Riding through Wyoming in the winter is tough."

Chuckling, Caleb nodded. "I know."

"Do you ever regret leaving the Rangers?"

The question surprised Caleb. He had many regrets. Quitting the Rangers after Regina's death wasn't one of them. "No. If my fiancée hadn't been murdered, I might still be living in Austin."

Dom nodded, as if he understood. Looking up, his gaze landed on a young woman strolling on the boardwalk across the street. He watched until she slipped inside the boardinghouse.

"Do you still have an interest in Tabitha Beekman?"

"I guess you haven't heard."

Caleb tilted his head. "Heard what?"

"A man she's known all her life sent her a letter with money for passage back home. He proposed. She's leaving town to join him." His lips tilted into a sardonic smile. "Seems I didn't move fast enough."

Caleb grinned along with him. "You don't seem too bothered by it."

Dom shook his head. "There are lots of women and I've got plenty of time." Sending an appraising look at Caleb, the corners of his mouth twitched. "I understand May Bacon might be available."

The answer came fast when Caleb grabbed the front of Dom's coat, face etched in anger. "May is *not* available." Seeing a gleam in Dom's eyes, he let go, muttering a curse.

Dom held up his hands, palms out. "Message received."

Shaking his head, Caleb shoved both hands into his coat pockets, offering no explanation.

"She's a good woman and there are more single men coming west every day, Caleb. My suggestion is to find a way to make it permanent before you lose her."

May felt terrible. She missed Caleb and knew the tension between them was her fault. She'd had plenty of time to think through all he'd told her, the difficult decisions he'd made, the deaths he'd witnessed. She ached for all he'd suffered.

After he'd revealed his past, May had walked out, unable to comprehend all she'd learned. Days later, she still hadn't had the courage to face him, ask the questions which kept her up at night.

She'd spent most of the day with her father, Walter, and Ernst at the Pelletier's. Dilly had been more than impressed with the horse breeding and training program at the ranch, as well as Travis Dixon and Wyatt Jackson. Along with Luke, they were the two men most responsible for their success.

They'd stayed several hours, long enough for Dilly to purchase a horse for May and discuss the possibility of shipping several animals back to New Jersey. Quarter horse racing had gained in popularity each year and her father had been searching for an opportunity to offer competitive mounts. A partnership with Dax and Luke might be the answer.

At four in the afternoon, May sat by the window in her bedroom, hoping to spot Caleb. She'd spent much of the day building up her courage. If she didn't talk with him today, she might not do it at all. An introvert, she'd always shied away from difficult conversations. May couldn't allow herself to ignore this one.

Ready to turn away, her heart raced when Caleb stepped out of the jail, taking a quick look up at her window. For an instant, their eyes met and held. She raised a hand, comforted when he returned the wave. All too soon, he turned, heading between buildings to his house.

Letting out an unsteady breath, yet feeling better than she had in days, May began her preparations to face Caleb. Laying her best dress on the bed, she began her toilette, brushing her blonde hair until the long strands gleamed. After wrapping it into an appealing style, she slipped into a clean chemise and her most stylish dress.

Checking herself in the mirror, May pressed a hand to her chest, trying to calm the incessant thumping. She winced. It sounded loud enough for Suzanne to hear in the kitchen downstairs. Picking up the small watch pendant that had belonged to her mother, May saw it was close to five thirty. Enough time for Caleb to have prepared supper for Isaac and himself.

Ignoring the low rumbling in her stomach, she grabbed her coat and hurried downstairs, hoping to beg a biscuit off Suzanne. May tentatively stepped into the kitchen.

"Good evening, Suzanne."

Looking up from arranging meat and potatoes on two plates, she smiled. "Good evening, May. It appears you're going out."

She nodded, feeling heat creep up her face, certain her cheeks were turning a light rose. "I wondered if you might have a biscuit I could take with me."

Tilting her head, Suzanne's features softened. "You're welcome to as many as you want. Let me wrap a few for you."

May stopped herself from saying she only needed one. Perhaps Caleb would appreciate having a few for Isaac. Besides, she'd become used to bringing food when visiting him.

"Here you are. Make sure you bundle up. It's looking like snow again tonight."

Taking the covered plate, May smiled. "Thank you, Suzanne."

Stopping in the parlor to button her coat and carefully cover her head with a wool scarf, May took a moment to calm herself. Inhaling and exhaling several breaths, she pursed her lips, ready to face Caleb. Picking up the plate, she left before allowing herself enough time to change her mind.

Crossing a street still thick with wagons and riders, May hurried between the buildings. A familiar scene met her when she reached Caleb's street. Smoke trailed upward from the three wood stoves in his house. Soft yellow light shown through the curtains hanging over the windows.

Forcing her legs forward, May stepped onto the porch, swallowing the anxiety gripping her. Raising her hand to knock, she yelped when the door opened.

"May!" Isaac stood inside, pointing at her while looking toward the bedroom.

Looking behind him, her breath caught in her throat. Caleb walked out of his bedroom, shirt open, showing the same hard chest she'd been held against the previous week. She didn't realize she'd been staring until hearing Caleb's soft chuckle.

"Hello, May."

Shifting her gaze from his chest, she looked up, embarrassed to see the humor in his eyes.

"Hello, Caleb." She glanced down. "Hello, Isaac."

"Hello," he giggled.

Noticing Isaac wore boots and a coat, May took a step back. "It looks like you're going out."

Buttoning his shirt, Caleb continued to watch her, his grin never faltering. "I'm taking Isaac over to Sylvia and Mack's. They're going to take care of him while I go out for a bit."

Pain flashed through her as the meaning of his words became clear. Chest squeezing, she took another step backward. "Oh. Well, I won't keep you." Turning to leave, May stopped when a strong hand grabbed her arm.

"I was coming to see you."

Chapter Thirteen

May sat perched on the edge of the sofa, hands fidgeting in her lap as she waited for Caleb. His announcement about being on his way to see her had surprised and excited her. He hadn't revealed why he'd planned to go to the boardinghouse. Instead, Caleb asked her to wait until he returned from taking Isaac to stay with Sylvia and Mack.

She jumped when the door flew open. Caleb entered, brushing snow from his clothes, his gaze not leaving hers. Taking the few short strides to the sofa, he stopped, staring down at her.

"Do you want some coffee?" He glanced over his shoulder at the kitchen. "Or whiskey?" His lips twitched as he turned back to her.

A small smile broke across her face. "Whiskey would be fine."

Tilting his head, he cocked a brow. "Are you sure?"

"Is that what you're going to have?"

"I hadn't decided. But if that's what you want, then I can't let you drink alone."

Striding to the kitchen, he filled two shot glasses, carrying them back to the sofa. Handing May one, Caleb sat down next to her. Touching the edge of her glass, he took a sip, watching as she did the same. Hers was a smaller sip, as if testing the taste for the first time. Face grimacing, she swallowed the liquid, watery eyes looking up at him.

Before May had time to comprehend his action, Caleb leaned down, brushing a kiss across her lips. Pulling back, his amused gaze watched her. "Do you drink whiskey often?"

She shook her head. "My first time."

Taking the glass from her hand, he downed the contents, then finished his. Setting both glasses aside, he rested a hand over hers.

"What brought you over here tonight, May?"

Biting her lower lip, she met his gaze. "Why were you coming to see me?"

A low chuckle burst from him before his face sobered. "It's been almost a week. I've missed you, May. Seeing you through your bedroom window this evening, well...I couldn't wait any longer." He squeezed her hand, lifting one shoulder. "I wasn't sure you'd see me after all you learned last week."

"I wouldn't have turned you away, Caleb." The weary, whispered response cut into him.

"Why did you come to see me?" He shoved aside the hope May wanted to continue seeing him, not daring to wish for more than he deserved.

Her bottom lip trembled, stopping when the pad of Caleb's thumb stroked across it. "Tell me, May."

Nodding, she let out a ragged breath. "I shouldn't have left you last week before we had a chance to talk through all you told me."

"It was a lot to learn at one time."

"Yes, but you deserved more than me walking out on you." She swallowed. "I understand why you left your family to join the Union cause, and why you didn't return home. What you endured when your fiancée was murdered, well, I can't imagine the pain, Caleb. Although I might not have gone after her killers, I respect your decision to hunt them down. They deserved a merciless death for ending the life of such a wonderful young woman."

Caleb's brows rose. "You never met her."

"No, but you told me all about Regina." Her chest tightened. "You loved her very much."

His throat constricted, remembering Regina's laughing face, bright eyes, and accepting ways. "I did."

She nodded. "Whether you accept it or not, I believe you loved Sadie." When he opened his mouth to protest, she held up a hand. "Not the same as Regina. No one will ever be able to take her place." Shoving aside the ache in her chest, she continued.

"Your love for Sadie came from your shared sorrow and the unselfish way she nurtured you, brought you back to life after a terrible tragedy. Beyond that, she's the mother of your son, a baby she kept even when you'd abandoned her." She felt his hand tense in hers. "Sadie kept Isaac because she loved you, Caleb."

Pulling his hand from hers, he stood, scrubbing both hands down his face while pacing away. Eyes closed, his

149

heart pounded as familiar guilt clutched at his chest. Whirling back to face her, his features hardened.

"Tell me the rest, May."

Glancing away, she searched for the right words. Hands trembling, she gathered her courage and began. "I love you, Caleb." She drew in a breath. "I've known it for a while now. When you asked to court me, it was as if my every dream had come true. Then Isaac appeared."

May saw the flicker of irritation in his eyes and rushed ahead. "He's a wonderful boy and I love him as much as I do you. It's just I don't know where I fit into your life, Caleb. You loved Regina in a way you could never love me. Sadie held a place in your heart, whether you choose to accept it or not. Isaac is a symbol of what the two of you shared."

She glanced away, not wanting Caleb to see the moisture gathering in her eyes. Waiting a moment, she looked back at him. "After the women you've loved, and now the love you have for Isaac, I don't understand how you could still have space in your heart for me."

Picking at the fabric of her skirt, she sighed. "Regina was the love of your life. She was a wonderful young woman whose heart was yours. I don't know that I'd ever be able to measure up to her." A face filled with misery lifted to meet his gaze. "I'm not certain I want to try."

All the pain, the anger he'd felt, dissolved away. Holding out his arms, he took a step forward. "I do care about you, May."

The hope she continued to foster faded. "I know you care about me, Caleb, and I'm grateful for it and our friendship."

Caleb saw the future he hoped for begin to disappear. "You're important to me, May."

Standing, she walked to him and wrapped her arms around his waist, resting her head against his chest. "You're important to me, too, Caleb. So very important."

Leaning away, he cupped her face with his large, rough hands. "What can I say to make you want to keep seeing me?"

Watery eyes met his. "It's what you'll never be able to *feel* for me, Caleb. You're still in love with Regina." Reaching up, she wrapped a hand around one of his wrists still cupping her face. "Maybe you just need more time."

His brows furrowed. "Time?"

"Enough so you can truly love another woman. Enough so you can live with your guilt over Sadie. When that happens, I hope you'll still want me."

Big Pine, Montana

Chad Devlin gathered his winnings from the last hand of cards, pleased at his three-hour winning streak. He'd already earned enough to keep him going for a long time, allowing him to ride about anywhere he wanted. So far, Big Pine filled every need.

"I haven't seen this much luck in a coon's age." The older rancher banged an empty glass on the table, signaling for more whiskey. "Hope you aren't planning to stay in these parts long."

Chad's mouth tilted into a wry grin. "Might stay for a while. Might not."

The rancher muttered a curse, downing another shot of whiskey.

He'd chosen a table at the back of the saloon and a chair angled so he could see anyone entering or leaving. Chad never allowed himself the luxury of feeling comfortable. The quirk had saved him more than once.

"Where you from?"

He eyed the rancher. The man spoke way too much. "Around."

"You looking for work?"

Chad smirked. "Not if I keep winning."

The rancher chuckled, then quieted, the game moving forward without further interruption. After another two hours, Chad piled his winnings in front of him, gratified and relieved the other men had already left. He checked the clock above the bar. Two o'clock in the morning. He hadn't realized how much time had passed.

Sending a look at the saloon girl standing at the bar, the one he always chose, Chad nodded toward the stairs.

Giving him a sultry grin, she strutted to the stairs, waiting for him to join her.

"You ready, sweetheart," he murmured against her ear at the same time his arm snaked around her waist. "Because I'm feeling in particular need tonight."

She giggled, turning to kiss him full on the mouth. "I'm always ready when it's you, Chad."

Nuzzling her neck, he tightened his hold as they walked down the hall and into a room near the back. Kicking the door closed, the outlaw shoved her onto the bed.

"I'm glad you're ready, darlin', because this is going to be a real long night."

Splendor

May stretched, noticing the early morning sun peeking through the curtains of her bedroom window. She thought of her new job, excitement rolling through her. An instant later, it died.

Last night, her heart had shattered and she had no idea how to fix the pain. Caleb hadn't replied to her comments his heart needed to heal after Regina's death and move beyond his guilt over Sadie before he could love again.

Instead, he'd held her to him, tightening his hold until May had been the one to push away. She knew many couples married for companionship, having children, or for financial reasons. They were friends, respected and cared about each other. A good foundation for building a successful marriage.

May wanted more. She longed for the kind of relationship Sylvia and Mack shared. When together, no one could mistake their love or total devotion.

It had been a risk, ending the courtship until Caleb could decide the extent of his feelings. She loved him, and every instinct in May screamed he felt the same about her. But continued pain and guilt kept him from accepting his true feelings.

Deep and lasting love showed whenever he spoke of Regina. A faraway look shifted his expression, eyes glistened, and there'd be a hitch in his voice when he described her.

May knew she'd never compare to the vibrant young woman who'd owned his heart. How could she? He'd created a memory so perfect no woman would ever be able rise above it.

She needed to be loved for herself because she was worthy of desire and passion from the man she adored. May had no wish to displace Regina in his heart. She wanted her own space, the same as he'd given Isaac.

A knock had her rising. "Yes?"

"It's Sylvia."

May's brows drew together for an instant before her eyes widened. Padding to the door, she drew it open, holding it wide. Motioning Sylvia to come inside, she closed the door.

"You aren't dressed. Did you forget about our plans for breakfast? A celebration of your new job."

Despite the hurt in her chest from what happened between her and Caleb the night before, May's lips tilted upward. "I'm sorry. So much has happened the last few days, I forgot. It won't take me long to get ready."

She bent over a bowl on the table, washing her face before brushing her hair. When she turned around, Sylvia had laid a chemise and dress on the bed. Slipping into them and her shoes, she grabbed her coat and reticule.

"It seems strange to have three days off in a row." Leaving the room, they talked while descending the stairs, walking outside to a clear morning.

Sylvia's mouth twisted. "How is the chef treating you after the changes?"

"He wants someone in the kitchen who doesn't offer suggestions, who stays quiet and just works. I can only stay quiet so long..." May shrugged.

Laughing, Sylvia walked to an open table at McCall's and sat down. Giving Betts their order, she leaned forward, grinning.

"So, you must tell me all about your conversation with Caleb." Her joy faded at the wounded expression on May's face. Glancing around, she lowered her voice. "What happened?"

Licking her lips, May described the night before, why she'd ended the courtship. "I'd hoped he might dismiss my concerns, assure me he could love again."

"He didn't."

May shook her head. "Caleb cares a great deal, but love? He might never be able to open his heart to any woman. Not the way he did for Regina."

Betts placed plates in front of them, making certain they needed nothing more, then left. May stared at the food, as did Sylvia, her enthusiasm for celebrating her friend's new position gone.

Reaching out, Sylvia touched May's arm. "I'm so sorry. I know how much you love him. I also understand how awful it feels to realize the man you care so much about may never share your feelings."

May had watched Sylvia and Mack go through their own struggles, hoping she never had to endure the same disillusionment she'd witnessed on her friend's face. It had been heartbreaking.

Shrugging, May continued to stare at her food. "It's up to Caleb now. We promised to stay friends." She pressed her lips together, slowly raising her head, the despair on her face almost more than Sylvia could bear. "The truth is I'll never be able to watch if he calls on someone else and marries."

"He won't." Sylvia's determined voice gave May hope. "Caleb isn't interested in any woman except you. Once he's able to allow someone into his heart, it's going to be you."

"How could you know that?"

Lifting her fork, Sylvia scooped up a bite of scrambled eggs. "Caleb doesn't even look at other women. When you're around, you have his complete attention. When you aren't, he's constantly looking around, hoping he'll see you." She placed the food into her mouth, chewing slowly, then swallowing, pointing her fork at May. "After church, he almost exploded when he saw you on Dom's arm as he escorted you outside."

Brows furrowing, she again glanced at her breakfast, still not interested in eating. "Then why didn't he find me afterward?"

"Isaac didn't feel well, so Caleb rushed him home. Believe me, if his son hadn't complained of a stomach ache, he would've found you. Which reminds me. Isaac talks about you all the time. Isabella laughed about it when she described making lunch for him and Isaac kept telling her *May could do it.*"

A brow rose a fraction. "I could do what?"

Sylvia chuckled. "Anything, everything. You make the best pastries, cook the best suppers, and play all the games with him. The boy is smitten with you, as is his father. It's just a matter of time before Caleb realizes all he'll lose if he lets you go. Remember, he doesn't want to watch you being courted by another man as much as you don't want to watch him with another woman."

"Are you saying I should accept being called on by someone else?"

Sylvia shook her head. "Absolutely not. Although it wouldn't hurt for him to see you with other eligible men. Such as having supper with Mack, Dom, and me. Or being seen with Hex or Zeke Boudreaux. He just needs to learn how desirable you are to other men. Caleb is a smart man who's struggling with his past. Besides, Mack and I will be on your side."

May leaned forward. "I don't want to cause trouble between Caleb and Mack."

"You won't. Once Mack learns what happened last night, he won't let his closest friend lose his chance for happiness. It was the same for us. Caleb made clear he thought Mack was being an idiot and would kick himself later if he let me get away." Sylvia shrugged, a sassy smile on her face. "Sometimes you just need a nudge from the right person to see what's already in front of you. Believe me, Mack knows how to nudge."

"No tricks, though."

"May, I'm not talking tricks. All I'm saying is you can't hide in your room when you aren't at the restaurant. Caleb needs to see you continuing with your life, spending time with friends, being involved in the town." Sylvia's eyes brightened. "The ladies will be putting up decorations in the church soon. Several of the deputies have offered to help, including Caleb. Christmas is a week away, and like you, he already accepted my invitation to come to supper at our house. Dom will be there. So will Hex and Zeke. All that male attention will drive Caleb crazy. Then there's Isaac. That little boy isn't going to let you get more than a few feet away at Christmas, especially if you bring a tray of pastries."

Finishing her breakfast, Sylvia set down her fork, giving May a conspiratorial grin. "Yes, this could be a very interesting Christmas."

Chapter Fourteen

Charles waited outside the bedroom, not wanting to bother Clare, yet not ready to let her return to the St. James. The last few days of her recuperation had gone well. She could've left his house days ago, but he'd convinced her to stay, ignoring what convention allowed.

While she'd slept, he'd worked at the clinic. After several questions from Clay, Charles explained the past he and Clare shared, announcing his decision to never let her go again.

"I'm ready." She stepped out of the bedroom, the few belongings Charles had retrieved from her room at the hotel in a small satchel.

Walking to her, Charles took the bag, then set it on the floor. Taking her hands in his, he searched Clare's face.

"You don't have to leave. Stay here, with me." He couldn't bear the thought of returning from the clinic to an empty house.

Raising a hand, she stroked fingers down his cheek. "You know I can't. Now that I'm healed, it wouldn't be proper."

He didn't know why he couldn't say the words, ask Clare to marry him and put an end to their misery. Charles had loved her his entire life, never believing he'd get a second chance. There had been a couple other women, but none who stole his heart the way she had. He'd chosen to stay a bachelor, putting all his time into his work. A lifetime alone. He found it more difficult than expected to say the words.

"Then stay a few more days, Clare. You don't have to leave today."

She waited, hoping he'd ask the question she longed to hear. When he didn't, she shook her head. "It won't be any easier in a few days."

Shoulders slumping, he reached down to grasp the satchel. "If you're certain."

She gave a reluctant nod. "It's for the best, Charles." It wasn't, but that was what she had to believe.

"All right."

Leaving the house, she slid her arm through his, praying he'd say the words that would make her stay. Slipping between the buildings, they crossed the street to the St. James.

It shouldn't bother her as much as it did. Having finally found the man who should've been her husband, Clare wouldn't be leaving Splendor. They'd share meals, go on buggy rides, and attend church. It wouldn't be as if they wouldn't be together, just not as she'd hoped.

Entering the hotel, he accompanied her upstairs to her room, stopping outside the door. Taking the key from her hand, Charles unlocked and pushed the door open before stepping aside. Knowing he couldn't follow her, Clare reached out, taking the satchel.

"Thank you for everything, Charles. Will I see you for supper?"

Clearing his throat, he nodded. "I'll call for you after I leave the clinic." Leaning forward, he kissed her cheek. "If you need anything..." His voice faded as he straightened.

Letting out a slow breath, she nodded. "Well, I should let you go."

Gripping the door, she moved to close it as Charles turned to leave. An instant later, his hand slapped against the door, stopping it just before it clicked shut.

Moving past her, Charles grasped her shoulders. "I'm sorry, but I can't let you go, not even a block away." He locked his determined gaze on hers. "I love you. Marry me, Clare."

Tears sprung to her eyes, a sob lodging in her throat.

Worry etched Charles's face. "What's wrong, sweetheart?"

Shaking her head, she swiped at the moisture on her face. "I've waited so long to hear those words." Fighting another sob, Clare slid her arms around his neck, nodding. "I love you so much, Charles. Yes, I'll marry you."

The man stood in the shadows of an alcove several rooms away from Clare's. The touching scene he'd witnessed meant nothing to him. Except the revelation of their impending marriage would make his job harder.

They should've snuck into the doctor's house and poisoned her. Or smothered Clare in her sleep. He'd argued about not waiting, getting it done, but his thoughts had been cast aside, as always.

New plans had to be made. The doctor and Clare were going to marry, and by the looks of them, he didn't believe they'd wait long. Well, he couldn't wait long, either.

They'd been stuck in this frontier outpost for too long already. Finally, they could see an end to their months of planning. It wouldn't be as easy as they'd first discussed, but the rewards would be beyond anything the two had expected.

Waiting until the couple disappeared inside her room, he let out a slow breath, stepping out of the alcove. His mind whirled at the possibilities for taking the life of the only person standing in the way of all their dreams. Taking the stairs to the next floor, he mentally thought about what needed to be done. Quick, quiet, and with absolutely no trace. That was how he'd take the life of stately Clare Billings without a bit of remorse.

Caleb strode down the boardwalk, stopping to talk to townsfolk and peeking into businesses while sending furtive glances at the boardinghouse.

The discussion with May the night before left him cold, empty in a way he hadn't experienced since losing Regina. Caleb wished he'd been able to deny May's words about his late fiancée. He couldn't. The pain of loss had lessened since her death, yet he still felt a piercing ache whenever he thought of Regina. He *did* still love her, would always love her, and if he were being honest, he had no idea how to get past it.

Worse, he still carried around a sizable amount of guilt over leaving Sadie without telling her goodbye, telling her how she might reach him. When he'd left the Rangers to pursue the killers as a bounty hunter, he'd let his ex-captain know his plans.

When the man requested he stay in touch, he'd agreed to send a telegram to the Austin headquarters every few weeks. Even though he'd left the Rangers, Caleb would do whatever he could for the man who'd taken a chance on him after the war. He hadn't given the same courtesy to Sadie. Hadn't taken a few minutes to stop at the saloon, letting her know she could reach him through the captain. A grave mistake he'd always regret.

Caleb had stared at the ceiling all night, unable to sleep, his mind drifting between Regina, Sadie, and May. The first two were dead. The last, very much alive.

Climbing out of bed long before sunup, he'd dressed, drinking three cups of strong coffee while staring out his front window. When Isabella arrived earlier than usual, he'd left for the jail, hoping for a glimpse of May.

After two turns around town, there'd been no sign of her. Remembering she had Tuesdays off, he'd expected to see her out running errands.

"Anything interesting this morning?" Mack caught up with him in front of the St. James, keeping pace as they continued along the boardwalk toward the boardinghouse.

Still glancing around, Caleb shook his head. "Nothing."

"Well, darn."

Caleb's brow arched. "You looking for some excitement?"

Mack shrugged. "Nothing big. I'd even welcome a few drunks we could haul off to jail."

"I don't think you're going to get that before noon on any day."

Mack snorted in disgust. "I suppose you're right." He glanced into the Dixie as they walked past. The lone customer slumped against the bar, his breakfast of whiskey before him. "Some people *do* drink before noon. Looks like Enoch Weaver is starting early today."

Caleb followed Mack's gaze, seeing the fifty-something man in his usual dark coat, white shirt, black bow tie, and flat-brimmed black hat. "He's a decent man. Too bad he's going to kill himself with whiskey."

"And he's a quiet drunk. I don't believe we've ever had to haul him into jail."

Chuckling, Caleb continued walking. "Like I said, no excitement so far."

Reaching the end of the boardwalk, they stopped. Mack didn't miss the way Caleb stared inside the boardinghouse window. "How'd it go with May last night?"

Caleb's features hardened. "Not well."

Turning away, they crossed the street, boots sinking into the melting snow and the deep mud below. The mucky ground wouldn't have been so bad if the sun hadn't burned down on town the last two days. Today, it sucked at their boots, making it hard to move around the numerous wagons and riders. Reaching the telegraph office, they stomped their boots on the wood planks of the boardwalk.

"How'd you leave it with her?"

Ignoring the ache in his chest, Caleb answered with a single shake of his head.

"Damn."

Caleb was about to say more when he spotted two familiar figures walking toward them. Sylvia spoke in her usual animated way while May kept her eyes focused downward, hands stuffed inside her coat pockets. When Sylvia saw them, she smiled at Mack, looked at Caleb, then glanced at May. He saw her head rise when Sylvia leaned closer and spoke to her. Seeing Caleb, her feet faltered enough for him to start toward her, stopping when she righted herself.

Sylvia stopped next to Mack, slipping an arm through his. "Good morning, Caleb."

Touching the brim of his hat, he nodded. "Morning, Sylvia." His deep blue eyes turned indigo when he looked at the young woman beside her. "May."

Worrying her bottom lip, she forced a small smile. "Hello, Caleb."

"May and I had breakfast at McCall's. We decided to have Noah saddle our horses so we could take a short ride."

"No." Both Mack and Caleb barked out the word at the same time.

Crossing her arms, Sylvia cocked her head at her husband. "It's clear and hasn't snowed in several days. If we don't go now, we might not get another chance for a while. Besides, May wants to try out her new horse."

Caleb, who hadn't taken his gaze off May, raised a brow. "New horse?"

Nodding, she tightened her grip on the reticule. "I forgot to tell you. My father bought me a mare when we rode out to the Pelletier's yesterday."

"Who trained her?"

Her eyes sparked at his terse question, but she kept her voice calm. "Wyatt Jackson broke and trained her. He saddled her and stayed in the corral with me until I felt comfortable. Her name's Calamity, and—"

"You bought a horse named *Calamity*?" Caleb's hard voice cut off the rest of what she intended to say. "Nobody marks a mare with a name like that unless she's not fit to ride. You'll have to take her back."

167

Crossing her arms, May stomped a foot on the boardwalk. "I certainly will *not* return her. She's sweet, feisty, and, well...I like her."

Clenching fisted hands at his sides, Caleb glared at her. "Before you ride out with anyone, I'll talk to Travis."

Teeth grinding, she shook her head. "You will *not* speak with Travis. She's my horse, Caleb. You're forgetting what we decided last night. You no longer have any say in what I do."

He moved closer, leaning to within inches of her face. "That was your idea, May. Not mine."

Feeling a flush creep up her neck, she licked her lips, lowering her voice to a whisper. "You know the reasons, Caleb."

His features didn't soften. "Which were damn fool ones." He hissed the words out, nostrils flaring. Realizing Mack and Sylvia still stood a few feet away, he straightened, releasing a frustrated breath. "I'll ride with you."

Seeing red flash on May's face, Sylvia stepped forward, placing a hand on Caleb's arm. "We both appreciate your concern, but there's no need for you to take time from your job to ride with us. May and I are both experienced riders. Remember, I grew up on a ranch in Texas, and May's father has been breeding and training racehorses since before she was born."

Removing her hand from Caleb's arm, Sylvia looked at Mack, lifting a brow. Seeing him nod, she turned back to Caleb. "Why don't the four of us ride out after church on Sunday?"

Caleb and May continued to glare at each other, neither responding for several long seconds before he spoke.

"Fine. After church on Sunday."

Sylvia clasped her hands together in triumph. "Wonderful. I'll ask Suzanne to pack food for us to take along."

Chest rising and falling with each labored breath, May fought the raging emotions fighting for space in her mind. The man before her was overprotective, domineering, and she loved him so much it hurt.

"If you're still interested, Sylvia, I'd like to take a short ride today." She sent a quick warning glance at Caleb. "Calamity needs to get used to me."

"I'd love to. Let's both change and meet at the livery."

Giving a terse nod, May said her goodbyes, giving Caleb a searching look before picking up her skirts and walking across the street.

He watched until May disappeared inside the boardinghouse.

"Well, that went a little better than I expected."

Caleb shot a questioning glance at Sylvia before his mouth rose at the corners. "You're right. It could've been worse."

"I'd better go change. I'll leave you gentlemen to your job of protecting the town." Placing her hands on

Mack's shoulders, Sylvia rose to her toes, kissing him on the cheek. "We won't be gone long."

"Please keep a close watch on Calamity, Sylvia. I know Wyatt wouldn't have let May take the mare if he wasn't certain she could handle the horse. Still..."

Hearing the slight tremble in his voice, she nodded. "I will, Caleb."

Scrubbing a hand down his face, Caleb stood on the edge of the boardwalk, watching Noah hand the reins to the women. The fear at May riding out on the young horse wrapped around him as tight as a noose.

"They're going to be fine." Mack stood by his side, waiting while the women mounted and reined the horses east. "They're going as far as Gabe's house. They'll take the trail around it before riding back. I'll bet they won't be gone longer than an hour."

Mack's words couldn't stop the dread clutching at Caleb's chest. He couldn't understand the depth of emotion pulsing through him.

Something ate at him, and it wasn't the mare. There was a soul-deep terror slowly building within him, warning Caleb to guard those he loved. It was irrational, frustrating, but no less urgent than the gut sensations he used to have during the war, or those which had saved him numerous times as a Texas Ranger.

The sense of unease was as real as May, the woman who'd wrapped herself around his heart, becoming a part of his life with unexpected ease. Caleb stilled on the thought. Did this mean he loved her? He hadn't thought so, had dismissed the idea with brutal effort. She was a wonderful, beautiful woman he cared a great deal about. But love? The idea punched him in the gut.

Unlike Mack before he met Sylvia, Caleb did believe a man could love again. He *wanted* to love again, spend his life with a woman who meant everything to him. Only one woman came to mind on that thought. May.

No matter how much Caleb fought it, Regina's image faded a little more each day until there were times he couldn't remember her beautiful hair and flashing eyes. Before May, he hadn't wanted to forget Regina, even clinging to the pain of her death as if it grounded him in some odd way.

After last night, hearing May describe the obstacles between them in such a calm way, Caleb knew he had choices to make, ghosts to purge from his life.

Steeling his resolve, Caleb headed toward the jail, a new purpose burning inside him. He'd never been a quitter and refused to give up now. Under no circumstances would May belong to another man. She belonged to him, and that simply wasn't negotiable.

Chapter Fifteen

Charles escorted Clare into the Eagle's Nest, hand on the small of her back. Pulling out a chair for her, he lowered himself into another, letting out a weary breath. They'd eaten breakfast, missing lunch to hurry around town, finalizing plans. It wasn't until Clare's stomach rumbled as they climbed the steps of the St. James that both realized their hunger.

"We accomplished a great deal today, sweetheart." He studied her face, still having a hard time believing the woman he'd loved his entire life would be his tomorrow.

"You were right. Reverend and Mrs. Paige are a delightful couple. I'm so pleased he agreed to perform the ceremony."

Charles reached over, patting Clare's hand. "Are you certain the simple gold band is what you want? We can put off the ceremony and travel to Big Pine."

The corners of her mouth slid into a mischievous smile. "I'd marry you without a ring. Unless you're having second thoughts. If so..." Her voice faded at the look of horror on his face.

"We are *not* delaying our wedding any longer," he grumbled. "I've waited a lifetime for you, Clare. I'll not wait any longer."

She bit back a smile. After all this time, she still saw the same familiar expressions on his dear face. The years had been kind to him. Charles didn't have the sagging jowls or growing belly of so many men in their forties. Trim, with a hint of silver in his dark blond hair, he was still the most handsome man she'd ever seen. And tomorrow, he'd be hers.

"I thought I saw you two. Are all the arrangements made?" Lena Evans took a seat next to Clare.

"We've done all we know to do." Charles ticked off their stops. "Spoken to Reverend Paige, picked a wedding ring, sent word to Rachel, obtained a license, and selected a dress for Clare, which Allie Coulter is altering."

"And arranged a late lunch for the guests with you." Clare smiled at Lena. "Thank you so much for being so wonderful about reserving the restaurant for us."

Lena returned the smile. She wouldn't tell them the partners in the hotel and restaurant would be paying for the wedding feast. Charles would object. This way was so much easier. He simply wouldn't be given a bill for the food and service.

"I assume you haven't eaten." Lena stood. "You'll be our first supper customers today. What may I bring you?"

Clare rested her weary body against the back of the chair, although her eyes were still bright with excitement. "Whatever is convenient would be fine with me."

The corners of Charles's eyes crinkled at the expectant expression on Clare's face. "The same for me, Lena. Thank you."

"I'm glad we're having a small wedding, Charles."

"It was easy once we made the decision to marry tomorrow. There isn't enough time to take out notices. The important people will be here, and that's what matters."

"How many do you expect will attend?"

"Thirty, at most."

They looked up when Lena approached with two plates filled with venison steak, potatoes, cooked cabbage, and buttermilk cornbread. "Here you are. Let me know if you want more."

"Thank you, Lena." Clare didn't wait to alleviate her hunger with the wonderful smelling food. She'd eaten here every day before the fire, but the food never tasted as good as it did today. Nothing had ever been as good as it was today. For the first time in many years, Clare looked forward to tomorrow and a shared future with Charles.

Rushing up the stairs from his spot in the lobby of the St. James, he cursed under his breath. Unlocking the door to the room next to his, he shoved it open.

"They're marrying tomorrow. We have to do something tonight." He lowered himself into a chair by the window. "Did you hear me?"

"Yes."

The one word response infuriated him. "What should we do?"

"If people in town are aware the wedding is tomorrow, propriety dictates she stay in her room at the hotel tonight. After she falls to sleep, you'll have plenty of time to sneak inside. You'll use her pillow."

"To smother her?" he asked.

"Of course. When you're finished, return the pillow to its place and leave the room. It'll appear she died in her sleep. Neat, clean, and final."

He chuckled at the simple solution. So much easier than burning down the church or trying to sneak into the doctor's house. "All right."

"Good. Now, you must leave. I must prepare for this evening's supper and pack for tomorrow."

His brows furrowed. "Pack?"

"Of course. Once she's dead, there'll be no reason to stay in this hovel any longer. We'll wait long enough for the doctor to provide the needed certificate, then be gone."

A broad smile broke across his face. "It can't come soon enough for me."

"Nor me."

Outside the jail, Hex pushed onto the back two legs of the chair. Bundled in his heaviest coat, his hands shook with cold as he whittled a piece of wood. A late afternoon wind had swept off the mountains to blanket Splendor in a bone clenching chill. The sound of boots pounding on the boardwalk had him lowering the knife and wood to his lap.

"Evening, Dom."

Glancing down at Hex's handiwork, he smiled. "Evening."

"Pull up a chair." Hex nodded at the one several feet away.

"What are you working on?" Dom leaned back in the chair, shooting a look at the piece of wood and knife.

"A horse for Isaac." Hex chuckled. "The boy wants a real one. This will have to do until he grows a bit more. Are you planning to stay around a while?"

Dom nodded. "I'm considering it."

Hands stilling, Hex's attention fixed on him. "That so? I thought once Tabitha Beekman leaves you wouldn't be far behind, heading back to Austin and your Ranger job."

Lifting a shoulder, his expression didn't change. "Neil Howie has resigned as the U.S. Marshal for the Montana Territory district."

"I hadn't heard about it."

"I doubt there's been any announcement. His last day is December thirty-first and they're still looking for a replacement. I met with him in Big Pine on my way back to Splendor."

Resting his hands in his lap, Hex's gaze settled on Dom. "Sounds like you're going to be the new Marshal."

"I'm not certain yet, so don't let that get around. Howie sent a telegram to Washington, recommending me. You never know what those officials back east will decide. Besides, I'm looking at buying a piece of land east of town."

Hex's brows rose as he blew out a low whistle. "Buying property is a pretty permanent decision for a man from Texas."

Dom stared at the passing wagons on the main street, mouth twisting in thought. "Sylvia is here. If I return to Texas, my father will put the same pressure on me to marry he did on my sister. I'm not interested in anyone picking my bride but me."

"So you're thinking of being a lawman rancher."

Barking out a laugh, Dom nodded. "Guess I might be. Depends on what I hear from Howie. I'm pretty set on buying the land and running some cattle."

"Did I hear you say you're going to run cattle, Dom?" Caleb had stepped out of the jail, leaning a shoulder against the building, hands shoved in his coat pockets.

"I'm talking to Horace Clausen about some land east of the Pelletier place."

"Do Dax and Luke know it's for sale?" Caleb asked.

"They turned it down. Clausen said they're not ready to expand any more right now."

Hex glanced up from his whittling. "You might also be looking at the next U.S. Marshal for Montana."

Caleb raised a brow. "That so?"

Dom nodded. "The current one is retiring the end of the month. He sent my name to Washington."

"I suppose y'all have heard the news." Cash joined them on the boardwalk, his gaze slipping down to watch Hex work the wood in his hand.

Caleb shifted to look at Cash. "What news?"

"Doc Worthington asked Mrs. Billings to marry him. The wedding's tomorrow at noon in the Dixie. The reception is at the Eagle's Next afterward. Lena says we're all invited."

Caleb remembered Clare, the woman hurt in the fire. "Do May and Sylvia know?"

Cash shook his head. "I don't know. Allie is sewing the wedding dress. That's how I heard about it."

Standing, Hex shoved the wood and knife into a pocket. "I think this news calls for a celebration. How about we all go to Ruby's Grand Palace?"

Holding up his hands, Cash backed away. "Sorry, boys, but Allie will kill me if I go inside Ruby's, unless it's to arrest someone."

Hex snickered. "Pathetic, but understandable."

Chuckling, Dom stood. "I'll go along. How about you, Caleb?"

"Wish I could, but I have Isaac." After what happened between him and May, he'd been hankering for a drink. Several would be better.

Hex moved next to him. "Ask May to watch him for a bit."

Caleb shook his head. "Not possible."

Dom clasped his shoulder. "If you change your mind, we'll be at Ruby's for a while before heading to McCall's for supper. Feel free to bring Isaac and join us there."

"Thanks, Dom, but not tonight. I'm going to spend the evening with my son and go to bed early."

Caleb didn't see a night in his future when he'd be able to relax with his friends over a whiskey while watching a show at Ruby's. Instead of the regret he expected, a grin tugged at the corners of his mouth. It happened every time he thought of his Isaac, the excitement on his son's face when Caleb entered their house.

The regret he felt had to do with May. He'd no longer have to wonder if she'd come by the house or join him for a meal at the boardinghouse. She wouldn't. They were over, and no matter how much he wished it weren't true, he had to accept the reality of her no longer being a part of his and Isaac's life.

"We'll see you tomorrow at the wedding." Hex nodded at Caleb and Cash as he and Dom headed toward Ruby's.

Cash turned toward the jail. "I'm heading inside. I'll let Gabe know you're on your way home."

"Thanks, Cash."

Caleb didn't budge from his spot on the boardwalk. He wanted to head home, relieve Isabella, and spend time with Isaac. He also wanted to stay put, watch for May, needing a glimpse of her before leaving.

"Did you hear about Doc getting married tomorrow?" Bernie Griggs, manager of the telegraph office, hurried toward him, not waiting for Caleb's response. "The whole town is going to be there. I'm even going to close the office for a couple hours so I can see it for myself. I'd best get home. See you tomorrow, Deputy."

"Evening, Caleb."

He turned his gaze from Bernie. "Evening, Noah. Are you on your way home?"

"In a few minutes. I wanted to talk to Gabe first. Abby has a gift idea for Doc and Mrs. Billings and wants to know if Lena and Gabe want to join us. Are you going tomorrow?"

Caleb hadn't thought much about it. He didn't know Doctor Worthington well and had never met Mrs. Billings. "I'm not sure. I'll have to ask Gabe who he wants to stay at the jail."

"Dutch McFarlin is due back in town before Christmas. If he rides in tomorrow, I'm sure he'll volunteer to stay here." Noah chuckled. "I've never seen a man with a bigger aversion to weddings than Dutch." Shaking his head, he walked past, heading into the jail.

Still reluctant to leave his spot on the boardwalk, Caleb shifted to get a better view of the other end of town. Several people came out of the St. James, a group of men stood outside the church, others talked near the general store. He couldn't see May anywhere.

180

It was time to go home to the little boy who loved him without reservation. The little boy Caleb needed more than his next breath. May might no longer have an interest in building a life with him, but he'd always have Isaac. That would have to be enough.

Chapter Sixteen

Charles didn't want to let Clare go. They'd made two turns around town, and he found himself tightening his hold on her arm in preparation for a third.

"When we pass by again, we'll go into the boardinghouse for coffee and slices of Suzanne's pie. Will that suit you, sweetheart?" Charles wanted to lean down and kiss her, not daring while there were still people around.

He'd tried to convince her to return to the bedroom she'd been using at his home, vacating the St. James so they wouldn't have to move her belongings after the wedding. For a time, Charles thought she'd agree. Instead, Clare dashed his hopes, deciding it wouldn't be proper. It had been quite all right when the entire town knew she'd been recuperating from the effects of the fire. Now that most knew of her recovery, they'd need to live apart, if only for one night.

"Pie and coffee sounds wonderful, Charles."

A few more minutes passed in quiet companionship before he opened the door of the boardinghouse, escorting her toward an empty table.

The instant Suzanne saw them, she headed straight toward their table. "I understand congratulations are in order. I'm so happy for the two of you."

"Thank you, Suzanne." Charles met Clare's gaze, their expressions so intense, Suzanne couldn't miss the deep love between them. Almost feeling as if she'd intruded, she cleared her throat.

"May I get you coffee?"

Tearing his attention away from Clare, Charles nodded. "Coffee and pie for each of us, please."

"I'll be right back."

After Suzanne entered the kitchen, Charles took Clare's hand, his expression sobering. "After we're married, I want to visit my lawyer."

The comment was so unexpected, Clare jerked enough for him to notice. "Why would you need to do that?"

Kind eyes met hers. "To change my will, love. As it stands, Rachel gets everything, which isn't much. Still, if something happens to me, whatever I have should go to you."

She glanced away, catching her lower lip between her teeth. When Suzanne approached with their order, Clare offered a smile she didn't feel. Talking of wills and estates held no appeal, but if Charles thought this was important, he deserved to learn more about the estate Raymond had left her.

"Thank you, Suzanne. The pie looks wonderful."

"You'll have to tell me what you think, Clare. I'll leave you two alone. Let me know when you're ready for more coffee, or a second slice of pie." She winked before walking away.

Charles allowed a few minutes for them to eat and sip their coffee before continuing. "I own the house, but the clinic was donated by several prominent families in Splendor. There is some savings, enough to live on once I can no longer practice." He grinned at her. "And the horse Rachel and Dax gave me when mine had to be put down. I realize it isn't much, but it should all go to you."

Chuckling, she set down her fork.

Seeing the expression on her face, Charles lifted a brow. "What has you so amused?"

"Nothing, really. Your comment just reminded me how little I know of such things as estates and wills. If you hadn't said anything, I wouldn't have considered changing my own."

"Don't feel you have to do anything because of me, sweetheart."

"Oh, but I want to, Charles. As I said before, I received a good deal when Ray died. Even though I provided a home and allowance for his mistress and their children, I knew he'd made separate arrangements for them outside his will. Ray had given his lawyers instructions that once I died, whatever was left would go to his brother, Harry. If Harry has passed, then the funds would go to his widow and any children. The lawyer said I could change those provisions in my own will. At the time, I saw no need. Now..." Her voice trailed off as she thought of their upcoming wedding.

"Don't you want to provide for his brother, Clare?"

After what she'd learned about Harry Billings, she couldn't find even a small amount of guilt at making changes to her will. "Ray and Harry had been estranged for years. In truth, I never met him during the entire time of my marriage. Harry had a, well...very unsavory past. Much worse than Ray's, which I found despicable."

Clare smiled at Suzanne when she refilled their cups and walked off. "After Ray's death, his lawyer provided more information about Harry and his widow."

"Widow?"

Clare nodded. "Oh yes. Seems Harry passed away almost two years ago, leaving a wife and son. Actually, the boy wasn't his. He adopted his wife's son, who was almost eighteen when they married. All of Harry's estate passed to his widow and her son."

Taking a sip of her coffee, Clare set down the cup, leaning toward Charles. "According to Ray's lawyer, Harry's widow married a wealthy widower from New Jersey a few months ago. So I really see no need to provide anything more to the woman and her son."

Stirring a small amount of sugar into his coffee, Charles nodded. "I do see your point, Clare. Harry's widow and her son have the funds from his estate and are now provided for by her new husband."

"I'd like to go with you when you visit your lawyer."

"All right, my dear. He has an office next to the bank."

Clare thought a moment, her eyes narrowing. "Do you think we should do it soon?"

Charles rubbed his brow. "As I recall, he is leaving for Big Pine at the end of the week and won't be returning until after the new year."

"Then we should see him on Thursday, unless you'd prefer to wait."

Chuckling, Charles brought the cup to his lips and took a sip. "I'd thought of spending the day in bed with you."

A flush appeared on her cheeks. "Of course."

"He leaves on Saturday. We'll take care of our business Friday morning. Agreed?"

Still feeling the heat on her face, an impish grin tilted up the corners of her mouth. "Agreed."

May needed sleep, but the same as the night before, it wouldn't come. She couldn't get Caleb out of her thoughts or her heart, wondering how much time would pass before she could forget him. She fretted it wouldn't be soon.

Turning to her side, May thought of all she had to do before the wedding tomorrow. The lunch Lena planned for Charles and Clare included several of her pastries. She'd need to rise well before sunup in order to prepare, bake, and arrange the sweets on platters before attending the wedding. And due to the large amount of food required, May would be assisting Gary with the rest of the meal.

Sitting up, she picked up her pillow, throwing it across the room in frustration. Groaning at such an immature action, May slid out of bed, plodding to the window. Drawing back the curtain, she stared at a cloudless sky dotted with millions of bright stars, fighting the urge to glance in the direction of Caleb's house.

She hadn't seen him all day, believing it best to keep her distance. When Sylvia went through the hard times with Mack, her friend admitted to enduring a crippling ache, sleepless nights, and a lack of appetite. Unlike her and Caleb, they were able to close the distance between them and marry.

Pressing a hand to her chest, she felt a single tear slide down her cheek. It could be years before Caleb put his fiancée's death behind him, finding room in his heart for another woman. There was the chance he might never get over Regina. There was an equal chance May simply wasn't the woman who could make him forget, capture his heart the way he'd captured hers. The last felt as if a knife had been plunged into her chest, causing her to double over.

Turning from the window, she slumped into a large, overstuffed chair. May wrapped her arms around her waist, curling into a ball while chastising herself for allowing emotions to cause such distress.

She had to get control of herself or she'd never be able to forget Caleb and meet someone who could love her. A man who could offer her the life she'd always dreamed about. Marriage, children, a small home with a garden, maybe a few chickens.

Closing her eyes, she drifted off to sleep, an image of chasing chickens out of her garden stuck in her mind.

It had taken an entire evening of waiting, hiding in one of the alcoves of the hotel lobby before getting his chance. Checking his pocket watch, he groaned at the time. A few minutes before midnight. He thought the young man at the front desk would never close for the night.

His chance came when the young man cleaned off the desk and tucked everything into drawers before making his way through the dining room and into the kitchen.

Unable to contain his excitement, he ran to the desk, opening a drawer. He pulled out a wooden box while keeping watch on the kitchen door. Rummaging around, he picked up and set down several keys before finding the one he wanted. Palming it, he shoved the box back into place and closed the drawer.

Voices from the direction of the kitchen had him hurrying away, dashing up the stairs to his room. Closing the door, he leaned against it, sucking in a deep breath. Another few seconds and he might've been caught.

Walking to the table beside his bed, he picked up a single piece of paper, scanning the list. They were running out of time. He couldn't miss a step or their second attempt to kill Clare might fail, and they might not get a third chance.

Checking the time once more, he opened the door into the hall, looking each direction to make certain no one was about. Glancing down at the key in his hand, he walked the short distance to Clare's room. He saw no light coming from under her door, but he hadn't expected to. At this hour, most everyone was asleep.

Sweat beaded on his forehead as he slipped the key into the lock. A damp hand turned the knob, releasing the catch. Shoving aside the hard ball of fear in his chest, he slowly pushed the door open, thankful the few lamps in the hall gave off little light.

Slipping inside, he silently closed the door before making his way across the room to the bed. All he could hear was Clare's soft breathing. She lay on her back, head turned away from him, resting on one of two pillows.

His heart pounded painfully, certain if Clare were awake, she'd be able to hear it. Holding his breath, he reached across her, gripping the other pillow. Slowly, so as not to wake her, he held it above her head, lowering it quickly over her face when she shifted a little toward him.

He hadn't expected the way her body bucked under his hold. Crawling onto the bed, he straddled her legs, pushing harder, feeling sweat drip down his forehead to fall into his eyes. Ignoring the discomfort, he used all the strength he possessed, groaning under the effort.

After a moment, her body stilled. He let out a ragged, almost giddy breath. He'd done it.

Rising, he climbed off the bed, unable to keep his hands from shaking. Looking down at Clare's still form, the reality of what he'd done settled over him. Voices from the hall had him whirling around, fear gripping him. He'd left the door ajar.

Taking one last look over his shoulder at Clare, he hurried to the door, gently pulling it open. To his relief, the voices had faded. Peeking into the hall, he glanced in both directions, seeing no one. Stepping over the threshold, his heart raced at the sound of people coming up the steps.

Swiping sweat from his face, he drew the door closed as two men reached the floor. Taking a couple steps away from Clare's room, he nodded at them, then turned toward his room. Before he could move away, he froze, hands fisting at his sides at the sound of a loud gasp from the other side of her door.

Eyes opening to slits, May frowned. Her back and neck ached, her body chilled to the bone. Glancing around, a memory returned of the night before. She'd fought sleep before curling into the large chair by the window.

Bracing her arms, she sat up, glancing out the window to the still dark sky. In an instant, May remembered the wedding and the pastries Lena expected. Jumping up, she rushed to the vanity, completing her morning toilette before dressing and leaving for the restaurant.

Ten minutes later, she finished tying her apron, thinking through all she had to complete before noon. May expected Gary would ask an unreasonable amount of work from her this morning, and she intended to do all she could. But it wouldn't be at the expense of attending the wedding.

Working without a break, she'd completed a decent portion of her work before Gary arrived an hour later. Giving her a curt nod, he pulled out pans, three large pieces of beef, several chickens, a large sack of potatoes, green beans, eggs, apples, and dried white beans.

"I'll need you to peel potatoes, clean and slice the green beans, boil several dozen eggs, and soak the dried beans. Afterward, I expect your help preparing the chickens." He didn't look at her as he spoke, the orders coming in a crisp, hard voice. "Mrs. Evans is expecting close to a hundred people."

May had already heard Lena's estimation. The thought of so many people celebrating Charles and Clare marrying gave her a rush of joy. She couldn't think of two people who deserved love more after so many years apart.

"Did you hear me, girl?"

Biting back a sharp retort, she nodded. "Yes. I'll start as soon as I prepare the next batch of pastries and the tarts are out of the oven." Turning her back on him, she busied herself, ignoring the man's snort of disapproval. Over her months working in the kitchen, May had learned the best way to work with the older man meant participating in as little conversation as possible.

The next hour passed quickly as the two worked at a rapid pace, May doing her best to ignore Gary grumbling his displeasure at how she completed her tasks. She had lived through his disapproval for months, knowing it would continue as long as the two shared the kitchen.

Hearing a sharp knock, May shot a look at Gary, wiping her hands down her apron as she walked to the door. Pulling it open, she gasped. Caleb stood outside, Isaac perched on his shoulders, his little hands grasping a wooden horse. Keeping her gaze on the boy, she focused on the new toy.

"What do you have there, Isaac?"

He held it toward her. "My horse."

"It certainly is a beautiful horse. Did you carve him?"

Giggling, Isaac shook his head. "Noooo."

"Hex whittled it for him." Caleb's deep, husky voice held a sad edge she'd never heard before.

Casting him a concerned look, she studied the lines on his face, the wariness in his eyes. "Hex is a very nice man."

Shaking the horse in front of him, Isaac's head bobbed up and down. "Uncle Hex."

"Did you come all the way over here to show me the horse, Caleb?"

Adjusting Isaac on his shoulders, she stilled as his gaze skimmed over of her. "Isaac wanted to show it to you."

It wasn't what she'd hoped to hear, but Caleb had never lied to her. She didn't want him to start now. Clasping her hands in front of her, May forced a grin.

"I'm glad you did. It's a very beautiful horse." Inhaling a shaky breath, she touched Isaac's hand. "Thank you for showing it to me. I need to get back inside. We're preparing for lunch after the wedding."

"Will you be able to attend?" Caleb's features didn't show how much he hoped she'd be there.

"It all depends on how much of the food preparation we can finish. I'd very much like to be there. What about you?"

"Dutch rode back in late last night. He and Zeke have volunteered to stay on duty while the rest of us go. They did ask us to bring them back some food." He grinned, although the usual brightness in his eyes had faded.

"Then I'll make certain to save some for them."

Caleb hesitated, as if wanting to say something more. Instead, he bounced Isaac on his shoulders, producing a giggle from his son. "Guess we should let you get back inside."

She nodded, not ready for him to leave but having no reason for him to stay. "Thank you for bringing Isaac by with his horse. I'm sure it won't be long before he has a real one."

"I suppose not." He gave her one last look before turning toward the street.

Feet rooted in place, May watched them leave, the feeling of loss so intense it stalled her breath. At some point, she knew Caleb would reconcile the loss of Regina and his guilt over Sadie. When that time came, whomever he fell in love with would be the luckiest woman in the world. She just wished it could've been her.

Chapter Seventeen

"It's so wonderful of you to invite me for breakfast." Clare looked around the table, warmth spreading through her at the friends she'd made in such a short time.

Lena, Suzanne, Sylvia, Abby Brandt, Allie Coulter, Isabella, Nora Evans, Caro Davis, and Ginny Pelletier had surprised her. Clare had thought it would be only her and Charles's niece, Rachel Pelletier. She'd been shocked to see so many familiar faces when she walked into the boardinghouse.

"We wouldn't have dreamed of letting you start your wedding day without a celebration. I can't wait to see your dress." Lena took a sip of coffee, all gazes turning toward Allie, who'd finished the gown late the night before.

"It's absolutely stunning. I dashed over to Allie's shop last night for a final fitting before Charles escorted me to the hotel. I couldn't be more pleased."

Rachel studied Clare, seeing dark circles and a weariness she hadn't expected. "Please don't take this wrong, but you look a little exhausted."

"No offense taken, Rachel. It has been a long few days of recuperating and getting everything ready for the wedding." Clare thought of the night before. "I didn't get much sleep last night."

"Too excited about the wedding?" Isabella asked.

"Yes, I am thrilled to be marrying Charles." Her face clouded. "But it isn't only that. The strangest thing happened last night. I woke in a panic and found it hard to draw a breath. It took quite a while before my heart stopped pounding." She didn't add how much the experience frightened her.

"Maybe it's from the stress of all you've been through," Caro offered.

Clare shook her head. "Whatever caused it, I was up the rest of the night." She glanced around the table. "The oddest part was finding my door unlocked when I left this morning. I'm quite certain I locked it."

Rachel's brows drew together. She thought of the fire, how Clare almost died trying to get out of the church. Now this. "It does seem odd. I know you have your mind on the wedding, but I'd suggest you talk with Gabe about what happened last night."

Waving her hand, Clare seemed to dismiss the idea. "The sheriff is such a busy man. I hate to waste his time on something as minor as being woken in the middle of the night."

"What about the fire?" Lena asked. "I can understand one strange event, but two makes me wonder if someone is trying to harm you."

Abby nodded. "Or possibly kill you. I agree with Rachel. Talk to Gabe, Clare. You really have no reason not to."

"Or I can talk to him for you."

Clare's eyes widened on Lena. "I couldn't ask you to do that."

Caro set down her empty cup. "I could always mention it to my husband, Beau, and he'll make certain Gabe knows."

"Thank you, Caro, but I don't want to impose on anyone."

"Does that mean you'll talk to him?" Lena asked.

Letting out a weary breath, Clare nodded. "First, I'll speak with Charles, ask his thoughts. But not until tomorrow. I don't want anything to spoil our wedding."

A light snow swirled around Chad, causing his horse to dance and whinny, sometimes bucking when the dirt became too thick. He'd been riding since well before sunup, making a quick decision to leave Big Pine for Splendor.

Chad never knew when the slow ache in his gut would occur, but he wasn't fool enough to ignore the unnerving waves of warning. Those instincts had saved his life more than once, and last night they'd come on stronger than usual. He'd played two more hands of cards, refused the offering of one of his favorite saloon girls to accompany her upstairs, and left.

Chad estimated he'd ridden over half the distance to Splendor when the pesky dust balls appeared. They were never pleasant, but these were particularly bothersome.

He already knew his belongings in the saddlebags would be riddled with gritty bits of sand and dirt.

He enjoyed playing mental games when riding alone. They helped pass the time and helped him recover from the usual hangover from too much whiskey the night before.

If he remembered right, today was Wednesday. The weeks in Big Pine had been restful, if not at all productive. He'd won a little at cards, spending most of those winnings on whiskey and women. Not once had he thought of robbing any of the banks in the territorial capital.

Sheriff Parker Sterling had a good number of deputies, all proficient with guns and offering little tolerance for anyone causing trouble in their town. Besides, Chad didn't have partners, no one to depend on to back him up during a robbery. He didn't need the money, but he did miss the excitement of riding into town, taking what he wanted, and hightailing it out before anyone suspected what he'd done.

Right now, Chad had no plans to rob the lone bank in Splendor. As good as Sterling's reputation, he'd heard Gabe Evans was better. He'd surrounded himself with ex-Union and Confederate officers, battle-hardened men who didn't panic under pressure. If the rumors were true, more than one of the town's illustrious citizens had been a sharpshooter during the war. Not good odds for a sole outlaw.

Reining to a stop, Chad reached behind him for his canteen. Taking a deep draw, he leaned forward, stroking a hand down his horse's neck.

"Won't be long and we'll be out of the wind and dust, old fella." At least Chad hoped so. Taking another swallow, he slipped the canteen away, picking up the reins.

He'd heard they'd built a real fine hotel in Splendor, maybe better than any of the ones in Big Pine. Chad didn't believe it. He couldn't imagine any sane man choosing to build a fancy hotel in a small, inconsequential town instead of the booming territorial capital.

It didn't matter. All he asked for was a bath, clean bed, decent food, and nothing identifying him as a man with an outlaw past.

Allie stepped back, checking the sleeves and hem one more time before a satisfied grin spread across her face. "I can't find anything else to change, Clare."

"It is stunning, Allie." Turning in a circle, she eyed herself in the long mirror. "I hope Charles likes it."

"I don't believe there's any doubt about that, Clare. Uncle Charles will love it." Rachel stood several feet away, as did the other women who'd been at the boardinghouse. "The green is a perfect color for your dark red hair."

Allie set aside her needle and thread. "It's almost time, Clare."

She turned toward the others. "I still can't quite believe this is happening. After all these years. I never dared dream..." Clare's words trailed off on a muffled sob.

Isabella pulled an embroidered, lace handkerchief from her reticule, holding it out. "None of that. You don't want Charles to see you this way. Why, he'll think you're unsure about marrying him."

Clare laughed through one last, ragged sob, dabbing her eyes with the handkerchief.

"That's better." Isabella shook her head when Clare offered it back to her. "You keep it, just in case you want to pull it out during the ceremony."

Lena walked to the front, opening the door. "Well, ladies. I do believe it's time to go to the Dixie."

"We need to surround Clare so no one sees her before the wedding." Isabella glanced at her. "It's bad luck, and we can't have any of that today."

"Are we ready?" Rachel glanced around them and stepped outside, leading the tight circle of friends across the street and down the boardwalk to the saloon.

Lena moved around Rachel as they approached the entrance, slowing her pace at the number of people crowded outside. She'd expected a good number of townsfolk would hear about the wedding and want to attend, but there had to be close to two hundred people, inside and out.

"What in the world?"

No one answered Clare's question, focusing their efforts on getting her through the crowd without causing damage to her dress.

"Do you see Uncle Charles?" Rachel glanced around the saloon, seeing her husband, Dax, and Ginny's husband, Luke.

"He's supposed to be with Nick and Gabe in the office. The rest of you stay with Clare until I find him." Lena excused herself, moving through the throng of people vying for space in the saloon.

The tables had been stacked in corners, extra chairs brought over from the Wild Rose, the other saloon Nick, Lena, and Gabe owned. From what Lena could see, every chair was occupied, each spot at the bar taken, and all available standing space filled. She'd expected a crowd, but nothing close to this.

Opening the office door, Lena slipped inside. "Oh, good. You're all here."

Charles whirled around, his features tense, mouth drawn into a thin line. "Is Clare with you?"

Walking to him, Lena touched his arm. "She is, and she's the most beautiful bride I've ever seen."

He let out a breath, the tension draining from his face. "Good. I was afraid she might change her mind."

Her mouth tipping into a grin, Lena shook her head. "Never. Although I do believe the number of people in the saloon shocked her."

Gabe moved next to his wife, putting an arm around her waist. "Is the place full?"

"Full?" Lena chuckled. "People are crowding around the doors because there's no space left inside."

Seeing the look of surprise on Charles's face, Nick clasped him on the back. "You've got a lot of friends, Doc. Appears they all want to celebrate with you and Clare." He looked at Lena. "Is Reverend Paige here yet?"

Before she could answer, the door opened and the minister joined them. "Do you know how many people are out there, Charles?"

He grimaced, tugging on the collar of his shirt. "I'm getting a good idea there are quite a few."

"I'd say close to everyone who lives within a few miles is here, my friend."

"What?" Lena's eyes grew wide, voice coming out louder than intended. "Are you sure?" She thought of the food being prepared, wondering if there'd be close to enough to feed so many. Lena doubted it.

Gabe drew her closer, whispering in her ear. "Don't worry about it, sweetheart. Whatever food we have ready will have to be enough."

She lifted her face to his. "How did you know?"

He kissed the tip of her nose. "Because I understand you."

Reverend Paige cleared his throat. "I suppose we should get started. Are you ready, Charles?"

He hadn't realized how nervous he'd be. Even knowing it was Clare didn't seem to calm the tightness in his chest or thickness in his throat. Charles hoped he could get through the ceremony without his voice wavering. Steeling his resolve, he looked at the reverend.

"I'm ready."

"Then it's time." Reverend Paige opened the door and walked out, waiting for Charles to join him. "You've nothing to worry about."

Charles didn't respond when his gaze landed on Clare. Releasing a slow breath, he couldn't look away as she started toward him, nor could he form a coherent thought.

A bright, unwavering smile lit Clare's face. Eyes locked on his, the crowd parted, allowing her to walk straight to him. He didn't notice her lower lip trembling until she stopped within inches of him. Reaching out, he took hold of her hands, threading their fingers together.

Turning to face Reverend Paige, Charles nodded. "We're ready."

May dried her hands on a towel, tossing it aside to grab her coat and reticule. If she hurried, she still might be able to watch at least part of the ceremony. Reaching the door, May stopped at Gary's gruff voice.

"Where do you think you're going?"

"The tables are set, the food is ready, and dishes are washed. I'm going to Doc Worthington's wedding. I'll come right back when it's over."

"Mrs. Evans isn't going to like it," he growled.

She gave him a gracious smile. "Mrs. Evans is who mentioned it to me. She said we're both invited. Why don't we go together?" May bit back a smile at the shocked look on his face.

Clearing his throat, he shook his head. "You go. Tell Mrs. Evans I appreciate the invitation."

"I will. I won't stay away long."

May bounded down the back steps, running to the street, coming to an abrupt halt at the sight of dozens of people outside the Dixie. She'd never seen so many people in town at one time. Disappointment slumped her shoulders. Not only would she be unable to watch Charles and Clare take their vows, she'd never find Caleb and Isaac. She felt a wave of guilt realizing the last was what she'd regret the most.

Moving forward, she got close enough to glance around the crowd and through the front window. All she saw were the backs of those standing. Frustrated, she turned away, staring down at the boardwalk as she started back to the restaurant.

"May?"

Lifting her head, she allowed a tentative smile to form at the sight of Caleb holding Isaac's hand. He looked so good with his chiseled features, indigo eyes, and charming, almost boyish smile. She waited as he approached.

"Hello, Caleb."

"We didn't get here early enough to find a place inside." He scanned the people flowing into the street. "I haven't seen this many people in one place in a long time."

"I was thinking the exact same. Doc Worthington is loved by so many. It seems every one of them wanted to be a part of his wedding."

They fell silent, moving aside as the crowd moved away from the door. A moment later, Charles emerged with Clare on his arm, the happiness on their faces causing a sharp pang of longing. May wondered if she'd ever experience such a deep, devoted love.

"I've never seen Doc so happy." May lifted her hand, waving at the couple as they walked past, getting a smile from Clare in return. "I need to get back to the restaurant to help with the food."

"I'll walk with you." Caleb swung Isaac into his arms. They moved at the pace of the rest of the townsfolk who followed Charles and Clare to the entrance of the St. James.

Stopping where May would turn to enter through the kitchen's back door, Caleb's attention landed on a lone rider. He'd entered town from the east, the direction of Big Pine. Reining his horse to a stop near the unfinished church, the man watched the large number of people huddling outside the hotel entrance, a thin smile quirking up one side of his mouth.

Charles and Clare had stopped at the top of the steps, turning to face the crowd. Clearing his throat,

Charles wrapped an arm around her waist, pulling her close.

"I can't tell you how much it means to Mrs. Worthington and me that you took the time to join us for the ceremony."

The combination of the stranger's hat tugged low on his forehead and the collar of his coat drawn up prevented Caleb from getting a good look at his face. Still, something about the man seemed familiar. A wave of deep unease settled over him, a nagging instinct Caleb knew shouldn't be ignored.

"Are you all right?"

Shifting Isaac to his other arm, Caleb looked down at May. "Fine."

She studied his face, sure she'd seen a flash of apprehension. "You don't sound fine. Are you sure nothing's bothering you?"

Taking another glance at the rider, he nodded. "I'm fine, May."

She didn't believe him but wouldn't push. "I need to get into the kitchen. There's a feast waiting inside for you, and a large table full of my pastries." Hesitating a moment longer, getting no response, she turned to leave.

He wanted to reach out, grab her arm, and force her to stay beside him a few minutes longer. Instead, he walked behind her, stopping at the base of the steps.

"When will you be finished?" The question came out before he could think it through.

"I should have all my duties finished by five."

"Is it all right if I come by to walk you to the boardinghouse?"

Faltering, she looked over her shoulder. "Why?"

Other than missing her, he didn't have a good answer, at least not one he thought she'd accept. "I don't like the idea of you walking home in the dark."

"But I leave here in the dark all the time, Caleb. There's no need for you to escort me." She gripped the doorknob.

"Let me to do it anyway." Shoving aside his pride, Caleb's anxious gaze met hers. "I miss you, May. I know you have doubts about me, but I need time with you. As much as you'll allow."

She'd missed him, too, hoping he'd seek her out as a friend if nothing more. "Well, I suppose it wouldn't hurt. I'll wait for your knock on the kitchen door."

Expelling a slow breath, he gave her a lopsided grin. "Isaac will be with me."

She returned his smile. "I didn't expect otherwise."

His features relaxed. "Good. We'll be here at five."

Walking back to the street, he took another quick glance at the rider. Another, more violent wave of unease clawed at him. He didn't recognize the man, had no idea where he came from or why he'd ridden into Splendor. The man could be looking for work or something else. Something more sinister.

What Caleb did understand was the overpowering tug of foreboding he felt as he watched the man kick his horse and continue down the street. He'd ignored the same sensation years before, and Regina's death was the tragic result.

Glancing behind him at the closed door to the kitchen, he thought of the woman inside, the only person he'd cared about since Regina. Never again would he ignore the unmistakable warnings of impending trouble.

Chapter Eighteen

Dax leaned back in his chair, laughing at some joke Luke made and Bull embellished. As much as he wanted to enjoy the wedding festivities, he couldn't get his mind off the strange killings of cattle at the ranch. It had been going on for several weeks, yet they weren't any closer to finding the animals, or people, responsible. He couldn't quite believe they had a pack of rabid wolves roaming the region, but so far, no other explanation made sense.

"For one day, can't you forget about the ranch and enjoy yourself? I don't want Uncle Charles to think you're not happy for him and Clare."

He startled at Rachel's question, not wanting their troubles to intrude on such an auspicious event. "I'm sorry, sweetheart." Leaning over, he kissed her cheek. "We should go rescue Charles and Clare from Dilly and Pauline." Standing, he pulled out her chair.

Rachel lifted her mouth to Dax's ear. "Uncle Charles did say how much he likes Dilly."

"And what did he say about Pauline?" He stifled a laugh when she crinkled her nose. "That's why we have to rescue them. Their good mood won't last long listening to her."

May peeked out the kitchen door for the sixth time, seeing Dax and Rachel walking across the room toward Charles and Clare. Three hours after the ceremony and most of the guests had already eaten, offered their congratulations once more, and left. Only a few friends and family remained. Not once had she spotted Caleb.

She'd been able to leave the kitchen for a few minutes to speak to the newlyweds and greet her father. May didn't linger long enough to speak with Pauline and Oliver, relieved to find them absorbed in their own personal conversation. Now they'd cornered Charles and Clare, Pauline doing most of the talking while her father gently tugged on her arm.

For an instant, May wondered if she should rescue the newlyweds, deciding to stay in the kitchen when Dax and Rachel approached. She watched for another moment before her gaze wandered to another man. Someone she'd never seen in Splendor.

He stood in the doorway, hat tilted back, and although tall, his heavy coat hid his true size. May couldn't tell if he carried a gun, but knew he must. Few people traveled without protection, and this man had the appearance of someone who'd seen his share of trouble. His presence caused an unwelcome sense of dread.

After looking around, he turned, walking to the front desk. She watched as he spoke to Thomas, the young man who most often registered guests. A few minutes later, the man glanced back into the dining room, gripping a key in his hand.

This time, it wasn't his appearance which prompted her concern. It was the predatory look in his eyes. The flat, emotionless glint unsettled May.

"If you stand there all day, we won't get out of here until late tonight."

Glancing over her shoulder at Gary, May tried to shake off her reaction to the stranger, finding she couldn't. Before closing the door, she took one last look, memorizing his features.

She and Caleb might not be as close as before, but that didn't mean he wouldn't want to know about the stranger, or anyone else who may be planning harm to those in Splendor.

Pacing back and forth in his room, Oliver stopped, placing fisted hands on his hips. "We can't wait much longer. Your idiot husband plans to have us on a stage right after Christmas. We'll never get another chance."

Pauline adjusted her skirt, settling into the only chair in her son's room. "If you hadn't bungled the first two attempts, we wouldn't have to worry about trying a third time."

"How was I to know Clare would find a way out of the church?"

"You should've stayed long enough to make certain, instead of running away," Pauline sneered. "The same as you should've stayed in her room long enough to know she'd never take another breath."

"Neither of those were my fault, Mother."

"Well, they certainly weren't mine."

Oliver slumped onto the bed. "I still don't understand why you married Dilly in the first place. You don't love him, and we had enough money to get by. We could've gone after Clare as soon as you learned about the contents of her late husband's will."

"I have no intention of just *getting by*, Ollie," Pauline huffed. "Besides, you know quite well that I didn't learn about his will until after I'd married Dilly. I didn't even know my late husband had a brother in Chicago. I always knew Harry had a good many secrets, but I never suspected a wealthy relative." Pulling a handkerchief from a pocket in her dress, Pauline dabbed the moisture from her forehead.

Oliver couldn't hold back a smirk. "Or that we'd be listed as Raymond's heirs upon the death of his wife."

"I'd have never learned about Raymond or Clare if Harry's lawyer hadn't mentioned them. Thank goodness Raymond had the good sense to send a copy of his will to Harry. If he hadn't, we never would've learned about the fortune awaiting us. We also would never have known of Clare's decision to travel to Splendor. I still can't believe our good fortune at learning both Clare and May would be in this town. You already know how easy it was to convince Dilly to visit his daughter for Christmas. He is a sweet man, but so gullible." She lifted the handkerchief, hiding her snicker behind the lace embroidered cloth.

Oliver's features sobered. "We still have to find a way to finish what's been started."

"Don't fret, Oliver. It's a week before Christmas. We have time to devise another plan. One that will result in us leaving Splendor with all we've ever wanted."

May tried not to appear anxious as she waited by the back door of the kitchen for Caleb and Isaac. Gary had already gone to his room upstairs, allowing her time to fix her hair before slipping into her coat.

At the soft knock, she pulled the door open, surprised to see snow blanketing the street. Caleb stood there, hands buried in his coat pockets, no sign of his son.

"Where's Isaac?"

"Sylvia asked if she could keep him for a bit tonight. So..." He shrugged, offering May his arm. "Are you ready?"

Closing the door, she slipped her arm through his. Neither spoke as he guided her to the street, watching as the snow continued to fall, covering the ground in a thick layer. Reaching the boardwalk, Caleb slowed his steps, doing what he could to prolong his time with her.

May looked up at him. "Did you have a chance to try the food today?"

"We came in for a few minutes to congratulate Charles and Clare. I ate some beef, but Isaac preferred the chicken. Both of us like your pastries. A lot, actually." He smiled, his eyes flickering in the light pouring out of the Dixie.

"I thought you hadn't been able to stop by."

He arched a brow. "Were you looking for me, May?"

Feeling her face heat, she couldn't quite meet his gaze. "Of course. I know we'll never be more than friends, Caleb. Still, it is difficult to let go of a dream. At least for me." Saying no more, she tried to pull her arm from his, only to feel his hold tighten.

He looked down at her. "Is that what you want, May? For us to only be friends?" Stopping, he grasped her chin, lifting her face so her gaze met his. "Because I want more." Bending, he brushed a quick, almost chaste kiss across her lips before releasing his hold. Had he not missed her so much over the last two days, he would've grinned at the shock on her face.

"I thought we agreed to give you time to sort out your feelings for Regina, and for me, Caleb."

"*You* decided I needed time, May. If you recall, I wasn't given much of a choice."

Looking away, she bit her lower lip, trying to recall exactly what happened on Monday night. When she thought of the conversation, May had to admit he was right.

She met his gaze. "Are you telling me you disagree with what I said?"

His hands moved up and down her arms, settling on her shoulders. "Some of it, yes. I'll always love Regina. She holds a special place in my life no one will ever replace." Caleb tightened his grip when she tried to step away. "You're wrong if you think I'll never be able to love another woman."

Another woman, but not me.

Refusing to look away, she lifted her chin. "Then I truly hope you find that woman, Caleb. You deserve happiness." Ignoring the confused look on his face, she twisted away, forcing a smile. "Thank you for walking me home."

May left him standing there, staring after her. But before she could enter the boardinghouse, a strong hand wrapped around her arm.

"I'm not letting you walk away this time." He stared into her wide, surprised eyes. "We're going to talk about this until we've figured a way to keep seeing each other or both of us agree there's no possibility of a future together."

Turning, he escorted her across the street. Walking past the livery, he followed the trail toward Gabe's house, then turned onto a narrow footpath. Loosening his grip, he lowered his hand to the small of her back, doing his best to control his body's reaction when he felt the sway of her hips.

"Are we going to the creek?"

Caleb moved his arm to rest across her shoulders, then stopped. Shifting to stand in front of her, he cupped

215

May's face with his hands, unable to wait another second. Lowering his head, he gave her time to protest or step away. When she didn't, he pressed his lips to hers.

He meant it to be a quick brush of his mouth over hers, enough to let her know she meant something to him. When she reached up, gripping his wrists, his mouth covered hers with an intense hunger, demanding a response.

Her lips parted on a moan. Powerless to resist, his tongue traced the fullness of her mouth, then plunged inside, his arms wrapping around her. He swept over the soft recesses of her mouth, igniting an aching need he'd never felt with another woman.

The thought caused his body to still. Easing his hold, he drew away to study her face. Slowly, May opened her eyes, staring at him in confusion.

"Is something wrong?" Her voice wavered.

He continued to watch her, taken aback at the way his body responded, his eagerness to continue. What tore at him the most was the knowledge he didn't just want her body. Caleb wanted everything she had to give him, already knowing he might never get enough of her. All this flashed through him after a few passionate kisses.

Regina's kisses had been loving and tender, but never sparking the fire he felt at the brief touch of May's lips to his. The knowledge shook him in a way he'd never imagined.

"May, I..." He didn't know what else to say. Nothing made sense to him. Certainly not the intense response, leaving his body aching and needy. "No. There's nothing wrong."

"Then why did you stop? Did I do something—"

He pressed a finger to her mouth, silencing whatever she meant to say. "You did everything right, sweetheart. That's why we had to stop."

Her eyes narrowed. "I don't understand."

Drawing her into his arms, he rested his chin on the top of her head. For the first time in his life, Caleb was thankful for their thick clothing. Without the heavy winter coats and gloves, it would've been too easy to continue what he'd started, knowing May wouldn't have stopped him.

She drew away, staring up at him, her eyes still glassy with passion. "What if I want us to keep kissing?"

He couldn't stop the deep groan or the renewed tightening of his body. The woman was killing him and she didn't even know it. "If we keep kissing, I'll be tempted to do more."

"More?"

Closing his eyes, Caleb didn't answer. Stepping away, he took her hand in his. "Come on. We still need to talk before I return you to the boardinghouse."

They walked another ten minutes before stopping a few feet from an almost frozen creek. A thin shell of ice covered the surface, the current underneath moving at a leisurely pace. Glancing around, Caleb led them to a fallen tree, helping her down before sitting beside her. Several minutes passed before he turned to face her.

"Do you care about me, May?"

Her brows furrowed. "You know I do. I love you, Caleb." May's voice held unwavering conviction.

"How can you be so certain?"

The corners of her mouth slid into a grin. "It's really quite simple. You're the most honorable, loyal, and dedicated man I've ever met. You respect others, and they respect you. You're smart and capable, willing to do whatever's needed to build a life far away from the comforts of your birth. I've never seen you shirk away from anything asked of you, never blaming anyone for a failure or accepting praise when it was due. Most of all, you embraced your responsibility to Isaac, giving him your unconditional love, doing all you can to be a good father. And one last reason. When you do find the right woman and fall in love, you'll never cheat or betray your wedding vows. You'll be faithful to your final breath." She took in a slow breath, her eyes sparkling with merriment. "It doesn't hurt that you're also the most handsome man I've ever seen."

He'd been overwhelmed with her unexpected praise, but the last statement had him throwing his head back on a bark of laughter. Removing his glove, he stroked his knuckles down her cheek.

"Ah, May. You are always full of surprises."

She tilted her head to the side, brows scrunching together. "I am?"

"I've never known another woman with so many hidden talents."

Shaking her head, she laughed. "I'm no more talented than any other woman in Splendor. Rachel is a wonderful mother and nurse. Lena runs several businesses and is a devoted wife and mother. Allie owns her shop, making beautiful dresses and amazing hats. And Sylvia can ride and shoot as well as any man, yet no one would ever suspect it because of her beauty and grace. I'm not beautiful, graceful, or have any talent in business. No, Caleb. My talents are slim compared to most of my friends."

Gripping her chin, his gaze leveled on hers. "I don't ever want to hear you say you aren't beautiful or graceful, because you're both. You're kind, sweet, and welcoming. I've never heard you say a malicious word to anyone, not even your pitiful excuse for a stepmother. You sew, cook, and bake pastries everyone in town agrees are the best they've ever tasted. And the way you are with Isaac..." He let out a deep sigh, unable to go on.

Releasing his grip, he took both of her hands in his. He knew what she wanted to hear, what he needed to say, but couldn't force the words from his mouth. The feelings he held for May had gone from deep caring to an almost desperate need in the span of less than an hour. Caleb didn't know what to think.

His gut twisted, confused at the thought he'd been wrong about his feelings for Regina. If it had been the deep love he'd always believed, how could his desire for

May be so much stronger with an intensity unlike anything he'd ever experienced? The thought of ever losing her chilled him to his heart.

"But you don't love me, do you, Caleb?"

He blinked, her question pulling him from his jumbled thoughts. Opening his mouth to answer, he shut it, not willing to say anything until he knew each word would be the truth.

Standing, May tugged on the collar of her coat, trying to stifle the cold, while forcing a smile. "I need to get back before Suzanne sends someone to find me."

Glancing around, he searched for words that wouldn't push her away. Standing, he reached a hand toward her, letting it fall to his side when she moved away.

"May..." Caleb stifled a curse. He'd never had a problem speaking with any woman. Not even Regina. But May had him tied in knots. "I need to be certain what I feel for you *is* love. You deserve nothing less. Don't shut me out, sweetheart. Allow me to keep seeing you. Please."

She opened her mouth, meaning to tell him *no*. Instead, she stared into eyes desperate for understanding. "All right, Caleb. At least for a little while longer."

Chapter Nineteen

Unable to stop himself, Caleb wrapped his arms around May, hugging her tightly. He held her for several long minutes, saying nothing, enjoying their closeness.

In a short span of time, Caleb accepted the truth. He'd lied to May. He *did* love her. More than he thought possible.

Pulling back, he kissed her once more, then took her hand in his. "Let's get you home."

They didn't speak on the short walk to town. It had started to snow again, falling faster and thicker the closer they got to the boardinghouse. He dropped his arm when they passed the livery, threading his fingers through hers.

Crossing the street, he stopped at the door to the boardinghouse. Moving in front of her, he stared down, waiting for her to look at him. When she didn't move, he placed a finger under her chin, lifting her head.

"Reverend Paige is having a special service on Sunday to commemorate the completion of the new church. Tuesday is his Christmas Eve service. Will you sit with me and Isaac for both?"

A slight grin tipped up her mouth. "I'd love to."

"Good." He bent down, placing a kiss on her mouth. "But I'm not waiting until Sunday to see you again," he whispered against her lips before straightening. "Come to the house for supper on Friday."

May lifted a brow. "Who's cooking?"

He pursed his lips. "I, uh..."

"You tell me what you want and I'll cook."

"Thanks, May. Don't bring anything. I'll have food at the house." He'd already decided to speak with Suzanne and buy the ingredients from her. Anything else he could buy at the general store.

"If you're sure."

A grin split his face. "I am." Brushing the back of his hand down her cheek, he followed it by kissing her once more. "I'll stop by the kitchen tomorrow." Reaching around her, he turned the doorknob. "In you go."

Caleb followed her inside, waiting until she walked up the stairs toward her room. Letting out a relieved breath, he headed home, his mind going over all he wanted to accomplish before Christmas. So engrossed in his thoughts, he didn't notice the man standing in the shadows near the land office. If he had, Caleb wouldn't have been thinking of May, but of the man who'd murdered Regina.

Chad had been shocked to see the ex-Texas Ranger turned bounty hunter in Splendor. He'd believed Caleb Covington had given up on finding him, satisfied he'd put Chad's two brothers in the ground.

Covington might have given up the search, but Chad had never forgotten the loss of his younger brothers. He hadn't planned to hunt the bounty hunter down, deciding it best to get away and start a new life.

His plans changed when he spotted Caleb in the crowd of people celebrating someone's marriage. Later, he learned it was for one of the town's doctors. He'd also been told Caleb was a deputy, one of several who worked for Gabe Evans, the sheriff he'd been warned about.

Even though Chad didn't believe Caleb had recognized him, he turned away from the celebration, riding down the street to put distance between them. If his face hadn't been shielded by the brim of his hat, Chad had no doubt he would've been discovered.

Tonight, standing out of sight, he watched Caleb with a woman who appeared to be special to him. Such a similar scene as in Austin several years before. Back then, Chad had noticed the Ranger with the beautiful young woman with dark brown hair, hazel eyes, and a smile that would melt the most cynical heart.

Chad hadn't meant to kill her, hadn't even realized she'd dashed across the street as the shots rang out from a brawl in one of the many saloons. A flash of yellow caught his attention before seeing a patch of red expanding on her chest. Stunned, he'd stopped firing for a few seconds. Long enough for a bullet to graze his arm, bringing Chad back to reality.

Everything changed that night. He and his brothers had left Austin within an hour, riding fast and hard, never returning. Chad knew the young woman couldn't have survived the wound to her chest. The three also knew the Texas Rangers would be after them. Especially one man. The same man he'd spotted in Splendor today. The bounty hunter who'd killed his brothers, gunning them down when they ran.

Chad had thought he'd put the anger behind him. He didn't fault Covington for coming after them. Any man who'd seen his fiancée gunned down would've done the same.

For a while, they'd thought Caleb had given up. Instead, he'd become a bounty hunter, tracking them to a small town in Wyoming. His brothers had spotted him, drawing their guns and firing. Chad would never know why they stopped firing, choosing to run. Their decision resulted in Covington planting bullets in their backs, killing his brothers instantly. Chad had ridden out that night, ending up in another small Wyoming town. The bounty hunter had followed him to South Pass City, leaving after a few days, as if giving up the hunt.

The old pain and rage returned when he saw Caleb with his new woman tonight.

Seeing the deputy walk between two buildings, Chad followed, being careful not to appear as if he trailed him. Curiosity rolled through him when Caleb knocked on the door to a small house, entering, then walking outside a few minutes later with a small child in his arms.

A feral smile tugged on Chad's mouth when Caleb walked into the house next door. This time, he didn't leave.

May bustled around the restaurant kitchen long before Gary arrived to prepare food for Thursday's lunch menu. She'd already helped him by peeling potatoes and readying the green beans while her pastries baked. As soon as he arrived, she planned to race back to the boardinghouse.

Tabitha would be taking the stage out of Splendor today to meet her fiancé. She, Sylvia, and Deborah Chestro, the other mail order bride, wanted to see her off. Afterward, Sylvia would return to her job at the general store, Deborah would finish cleaning rooms at the St. James, and May would head back to the kitchen.

Hearing the door open, she spun around, expecting to see Gary. Instead, a man she'd never seen walked inside, causing her throat to tighten. He was the same man she'd seen in town. The one she'd forgotten to tell Caleb about. Without thought, she backed away, putting one of the large preparation tables between her and the man.

"If you're looking for the entrance to the restaurant, it's through the hotel lobby."

Closing the door, the man took a few steps toward her. His gaze moved to her face, skimming down her neck to her chest, then to the curve of her waist before returning to lock onto her eyes. May's stomach knotted at his unrepentant stare. Glancing behind her, she estimated it wouldn't take more than a few steps to dash into the dining room toward the lobby.

"I'm not looking for the restaurant, Miss..." His voice trailed off.

"Miss Bacon. Who are you?"

"Just a man who's new in town and saw a pretty lady I wanted to meet."

Her eyes narrowed, unsure of what he meant. "If you describe her, perhaps I can tell you her name."

He chuckled. "I already have her name. Miss Bacon, correct?"

"Why would you want to meet me?"

Settling both hands on the table, he leaned forward. "Like I said, I'm always interested in meeting a pretty lady, and you're about the prettiest thing I've seen in a long time."

Trying not to panic, May moved slowly toward the door to the dining room. With each step, she chastised herself for not telling Caleb about the man she'd spotted watching the wedding festivities.

"You have me at a disadvantage, sir. You know my name, but I don't know yours." She inched back another foot.

"My name doesn't matter any." He straightened, watching in amusement at her attempts to get away from him. "Well, I should be getting along. It was good to meet you, Miss Bacon." He opened the door, slipping out an instant before Gary entered from the dining room, causing May to jump and turn around.

She placed a hand over her chest. "You scared me, Gary."

He didn't seem to notice the distress on her face or the way her hands shook. "Don't know why. You should've been expecting me."

Whirling back around, she dashed to the side door. Sucking in a deep breath, she opened it, peering up and down the path between the two buildings.

"What *are* you doing, May?" Gary's tone held a good measure of annoyance.

"There was a man in here. He came in the back door and, well..." She bit her bottom lip.

"He what?"

She shook her head. "His behavior was odd, almost threatening."

Placing clenched fists on his waist, Gary took a couple steps toward her. "What did he say?"

"Asked my name and..." She tried to remember what else, coming up short. "He didn't look right, Gary."

"If all he asked was your name, I don't see any problem." Dropping his arms to his sides, he stalked off toward the larder, pulling out what he needed for the lunch menu.

Heart still pounding, she forced herself to move toward the hook where she'd placed her coat. "I'll be right back, Gary. I need to see the stage off."

May didn't wait for a response before leaving through the dining room and out the front entrance to the hotel. Glancing around, her gaze moved across each person on the street and boardwalk. A rush of relief surged through her when she didn't catch a glimpse of the man.

Seeing the stagecoach, May lifted her dress and hurried down the street, waving at Sylvia and Deborah. She'd almost reached them when the driver slapped the lines and the coach lurched forward.

"Wait!"

May ran as fast as she could in her heavy coat, boots, and dress. Sylvia yelled to the driver. He either didn't hear her or ignored her shouts to stop. Slowing her pace, May waved at Tabitha as the stage roared down the main street, taking the trail east toward Big Pine.

"Well, darn." May sucked in a breath, disappointed at not giving her friend a proper goodbye. Feeling a hand on her shoulder, she turned, fearing who might be standing next to her. Looking up, she relaxed.

Dom dropped his hand, watching the stage as it turned and disappeared out of sight. "You can write her. Tabitha gave her address to Sylvia." The smile she'd grown to expect from her friend's brother didn't appear. At one time, May and Sylvia had thought he intended to court Tabitha.

"Thank you, Dom." Her words drifted unheard into the air. Dom had already left.

Walking closer, May tried to get a better look at two women near the stage stop. She recognized one as Nick Barnett's daughter, Olivia. Twenty-one, with hair as dark as her father's and green eyes, May thought she was

228

one of the most striking beauties she'd ever seen. Next to her stood another young woman.

"May. You must come meet Olivia's friend." Sylvia waved her over, smiling when Dominic joined her. "I'll introduce both of you." Stepping next to Olivia, she touched her friend's arm. "I'd like to introduce May and Dom to your friend."

Olivia's face brightened even more. "Of course. Josephine, this is Miss May Bacon, a friend of mine, and Dominic Lucero, Sylvia's brother. Dom and May, this is my very good friend, Miss Josephine Dubois."

May took a step closer. "It's so nice to meet you, Miss Dubois."

"It's my pleasure, Miss Bacon. Please, call me Josie."

"Then you must call me May."

Clearing his throat, Dom extended his hand, taking Josie's and brushing a kiss across the back. His eyes crinkled, seeing her face redden. "It's a pleasure to meet one of Olivia's friends. I hope your stay in Splendor will be enjoyable."

Face still flushed, Josie glanced at Olivia, who said nothing as she offered a smile. Regaining her composure, she gently pulled her hand free of Dom's grasp. "Thank you, Mr. Lucero. I've been wanting to visit Olivia for quite some time."

Sylvia shot a look at Dom, her eyes narrowing. Clearing her throat, she touched her brother's hand. "Well, we should be going. I'm so glad you'll be staying in Splendor, Josie."

"Do you need help with your trunk and bags, Miss Dubois?"

"Apologies, ladies." Nick dashed across the street, stopping next to his daughter, but looking at Josie. "You must be Miss Dubois. I've heard a good deal about you." He held out his hand, taking hers and giving it the same attention as Dom.

Josie didn't flush as she did with Dom. "Thank you so much for letting me visit, Mr. Barnett. I've been looking forward to this trip for months." A radiant smile brightened her face.

"The pleasure is ours. Now, let me get the buggy from Noah and I'll drive you and Olivia to the house."

Olivia touched his arm. "I do have my horse, Father."

Nick's face softened when he looked at his daughter. "Let's tie her to the wagon, *ma cherie*. I'm quite certain you'd like to visit with Josephine."

Olivia kissed Nick's cheek. "That would be marvelous."

Dom didn't want to leave, but Sylvia's insistent tugging had his feet moving. When they reached the boardwalk, he pulled from her grasp.

"Do you know anything about her, Syl?"

"Absolutely nothing, other than she's Olivia's best friend."

May looked behind Dom to see Noah lifting the trunk and bags into the buggy. "Do you think Nick is ever going to allow Doc McCord to court Olivia? Suzanne said Clay's been asking for his approval for months."

Sylvia bit back a laugh, lowering her voice so only May and Dom could hear. "It had better be soon. When I had lunch with Olivia before the fire, she confided they've been seeing each other behind Nick's back for weeks."

May's eyes flew open, while Dom threw back his head and laughed.

Sylvia slapped his arm. "It's not funny, Dom. Clay is a wonderful man, and he and Olivia love each other. I just don't understand what Nick is waiting for. Suzanne thinks they might run away to Big Pine and marry if he doesn't come around soon."

At the sound of the buggy, the three glanced toward the street. "Maybe Josie can help convince Nick to give his approval. Why..." May's voice stalled as an idea popped into her head. "You don't think Josie is here because Clay and Olivia *do* plan to run off, do you?"

Sylvia's hand flew to her mouth. "I hadn't thought of that, but you're right. Well, they won't be going alone."

Dom lifted a brow. "What are you planning, Syl?"

"That we accompany them, of course. We'll volunteer to be witnesses. May and I will stand with Olivia, and you can stand with Clay."

May pulsed with excitement. "What a brilliant idea. We must speak with Olivia soon."

Gripping their elbows, Dom escorted the women back down the boardwalk, his thoughts on the beautiful

Josephine Dubois. "I agree, Syl. For once, you've come up with an excellent idea."

Chapter Twenty

Charles stood in the doorway of their bedroom, watching Clare apply the finishing touches to her hair. After so many years alone, he'd often wondered how long it would take before he felt comfortable with a woman in his home. Within minutes of entering the house after their marriage, he knew there'd be no need to adjust. Clare fit as if they'd always been together.

Noticing her struggle with the necklace he'd given her as a wedding gift, he walked toward her. "Do you need help?"

She looked in the mirror, meeting his gaze. "Yes, please."

Gripping each end of the necklace, he secured the clasp before leaning down to kiss her neck. "We can always wait to see the lawyer until after he returns from Big Pine," Charles whispered against her ear, feeling her shiver.

Clare's head fell back to rest against him. "I could be persuaded."

Chuckling, he turned her to face him, pressing his lips against hers before stepping away. "Let's get this meeting over with, have an early supper, and come back here."

Her brow rose. "To finish what you started?"

Taking her hand, he smiled. "Of course."

Stepping into the cool afternoon air, he slipped Clare's hand through his arm, leading her the short distance to the law office. He stopped at the entrance, noting the new sign on the door. He touched the engraved lettering with his finger.

"Ernest Payson started a law practice here a few years ago. After his brother, Albert, came to join him, Ernest decided to travel back to Boston." He looked at Clare, his features drawn with sadness. "Unfortunately, Albert was murdered by outlaws this past year. We had all hoped Ernest would return to reclaim the practice, but didn't allow ourselves to count on it. One day, he came in on the stage, said hello to those who greeted him, and walked through this door as if he'd never been gone. Appears the new plaque finally arrived."

Gripping her elbow, he ushered her into a small waiting area. "The desk in front is never occupied. Ernest plans to hire a secretary once the practice gets big enough. Since just about everyone in Splendor uses him, I'm guessing it won't be long."

"Perhaps he's able to handle everything himself."

A smile spread across his face. "Wait until you see his office, then tell me what you think."

The glass in the door ahead of them read the same as the sign outside. *Ernest Payson, Attorney.* Knocking, he waited a moment, then turned the handle.

"Doctor and Mrs. Worthington." Ernest stood, walking around the desk to grip Charles's outstretched hand and make a slight bow to Clare. "Congratulations again on your marriage. I was one of the fortunate people who actually had a seat inside the Dixie. Please, sit down and explain to me what I may do for you."

Caleb paced outside the jail on Friday, unable to sit any longer in the hard wooden chair on the boardwalk. Supper with May on Wednesday went better than he'd planned. She'd fixed their meal, played with Isaac, and read to him before she and Caleb tucked his son into bed.

The instant they'd left Isaac's room, he'd taken her into his arms. Their kisses had continued until he scooped her up, settled himself on the sofa, and placed her in his lap. A while later, May pushed lightly on his chest, breaking their kiss.

It took less than a minute for the warm, tranquil feeling inside him to fade, replaced by heart-pounding rage. May's description of the man she'd seen on the street, the same one who'd entered the kitchen uninvited, could only be one man. Chad Devlin had ridden into Splendor, and whatever he planned wouldn't be good. Without revealing Chad as Regina's killer, he'd promised May to find out more about the man who'd frightened her.

Afterward, he hadn't been content watching her cross the street and head into the darkness toward the boardinghouse. Instead, Caleb locked the door and escorted her home, ending their evening with a long, deep kiss he knew would keep him awake for much of the night. That, and the knowledge of Devlin being in Splendor.

Rising early on Thursday morning, he'd taken Isaac to Isabella's, explaining his need to get to the jail early. He'd alerted Gabe and the other deputies, everyone taking extra tours around town, hoping to spot the killer. All they'd learned was a man meeting Chad's description had spent one night at the hotel, then left.

His gut told him Chad hadn't ridden out. Somehow, the outlaw had discovered Caleb's affection for May, scared her without making any overt threats, then disappeared. She might not have understood the message, but to him, the warning was clear.

"Hello, Caleb."

Spinning around at the soft voice, his breath caught when his gaze settled on May. "Hey, sweetheart." Taking a couple steps forward, he ran a hand down her arm, wanting to lean down and kiss her. Instead, his hand clasped hers for an instant before he let go. "I thought you worked early on Fridays. Where are you going?"

"Lena asked me to change my schedule today, which I agreed to do. Right now, I'm headed to the general store and to see Allie." She held up a package. "I need a skirt altered and can't find the time to do it myself." May glanced down the street at the St. James. "Father asked me to meet him and Pauline for a late lunch. He wants to talk with me before I go to work."

Caleb's stomach clenched as he thought about what might be Dilly's reason for the talk. He hoped it wasn't to persuade May to return to New Jersey. The idea forced him to think of Chad. Perhaps it was best she leave Splendor, return to a life less prone to violence, where she wouldn't be a target because of him.

"Do you know why he wants to talk with you?"

Shaking her head, she fidgeted with the package in her hand. "I'm not sure. Probably to try and convince me to return home."

"Is that what you want?"

"No, Caleb." She met his intense stare. "What I want is a life here, with you and Isaac. If that isn't meant to be, then maybe I'll consider leaving."

Body relaxing, he reached for her hand again, threading his fingers through hers. "I don't want you to go, May." If they were somewhere else, almost anywhere else, he'd admit to loving her, ask her to marry him. Now wasn't the time, but it would be soon.

Squeezing his hand, a hopeful smile tipped her lips. "I was hoping you'd say that." She glanced around, brows furrowing. "Why are you pacing outside? Is something wrong?"

Drawing her to the chairs outside the jail, he indicated for her to sit down. Reaching to the side, he moved a chair closer, never letting go of her hand.

"Gabe and all the deputies are trying to find the man who came into the kitchen. He stayed a night at the St.

James, then left. From what we can find out, you were the last one to see him in town."

"That's good, isn't it?"

"Maybe. It could also mean he's nearby but staying out of sight." His jaw clenched, wanting to warn May without scaring her. "I'd feel better if you didn't go anywhere alone until we find him, or determine he's left Splendor."

Eyes widening for a moment, she studied Caleb's face, seeing deep lines from either worry or lack of sleep. Maybe both. "I can't always have someone with me."

He leaned forward. "I think you can. When you're working in the kitchen, lock the back door and use the hotel entrance to come and go. I'll walk you to and from the St. James each day you work. When you aren't working, you'll be with me."

She jerked away, her voice rising. "What?"

He looked around, lowering his voice. "I've already talked with Gabe. He agrees you shouldn't be alone. If you aren't with me, you need to be with someone, May. Personally, I'd rather it be me."

Lifting a brow, her mouth drew into a thin line before she expelled a frustrated breath.

"Like now. I'll walk you to the general store and Allie's."

Her mouth twisted into a smirk. "Are you willing to have lunch with me and my father?"

"I don't think he'll do anything inside the hotel while you're with other people. But if you want me to join you, I will."

Her eyes lit up. "You will? That would be wonderful."

Stifling a groan, he nodded. He'd do whatever was needed to keep her safe. "All right. When we're done with lunch, you'll work in the kitchen. I'll be waiting to walk you back to the boardinghouse when you're finished. Tomorrow morning, I'll accompany you from the boardinghouse to the kitchen." He smiled, remembering her promise to have supper with him and Isaac Saturday evening. "Afterward, we'll go to my place for supper."

She let out a disgruntled breath. "What you're saying is my life isn't mine until you've found and spoken to the man, right? Not that I don't want to see you, because I do. But you know what some of the women in town will say about us being alone at your house so often."

He stroked a hand down her face. "If what they're thinking is we mean a great deal to each other, they would be right."

Mouth twisting, she nodded. "If you believe it's important, we'll do it your way."

"What I'm saying is *you're* important, May." Standing, he held out his hand, intertwining their fingers as they walked to the general store. "Just don't ask me to help pick out ribbon or fabric or whatever it is women shop for."

Laughing, she shook her head. "I'd never dream of it, Caleb."

"I'm so glad we met with Ernest, Charles. We'll both rest easier now that we've made our wishes clear. Are you certain it's best to keep the documents in his safe?"

Patting her hand, he picked up the handwritten menu for the Eagle's Nest. "They'll be safer there than at our house."

She nodded, a grin tugging at her lips. *Our house* was all Clare really heard.

A rustling noise at the front had them both looking up to see Dilly, Pauline, and Oliver. A moment later, May and Caleb joined them. Charles and Clare nodded in greeting. She leaned over to whisper in his ear.

"I'd like to visit with May and Caleb, but I'm not up to talking with Pauline. Not even a short conversation."

Chuckling, Charles nodded. "Neither am I, dear. We'll have to plan a visit with May and Caleb another time."

They ate in silence, talking in low voices while trying to ignore Pauline's grating voice. With each sentence, it rose until Clare felt certain everyone in the restaurant could hear her berating May, Caleb, and Dilly. As another minute passed without the woman stopping, allowing no one to speak, Clare had enough. Catching Charles by surprise, she stood, walking to their table.

"I'm sorry to interrupt, but may I speak with May and Caleb in private for a moment?" She glanced at Pauline, almost stepping back at the malicious expression on the woman's face.

"Certainly." Ignoring Pauline, Dilly smiled at May and Caleb. "Why don't you go with Mrs. Worthington? It will give me a chance to speak with my wife."

They followed Clare to her table, Caleb accepting the hand Charles extended. "Please, sit down."

May sent a questioning look at Caleb before taking a chair next to Clare. "Are you two all right?"

Nodding, Clare took a sip of her tea. "We're fine, May. I'm sorry to have interrupted, but I couldn't tolerate Pauline maligning you two and Mr. Bacon any longer. None of you deserve to be treated in such a disrespectful manner. Everyone in the restaurant could hear her. It wasn't right." Her hand shook as she lifted the cup again, took a small swallow, and set it down.

Reaching over, Charles covered her hand with his. "Are you all right, Clare?"

She nodded, her expression closed.

Glancing at Caleb, May looked at Clare. "I'm so glad you interrupted her. She's mean and spiteful. Nothing at all like my mother. To be honest, I simply don't understand what attracted my father to her. Please don't feel bad about saving us, Clare. We're grateful you did."

"She's right, Mrs. Worthington. If you hadn't come to the table, I would've left with May." Caleb looked past Charles to the table where Dilly spoke with Pauline, his expression cold and unyielding. "I sure hope Mr. Bacon sets his wife straight."

"Or leaves her," May muttered, staring across the restaurant at her father.

"I'll not put up with your constant harping any longer, Pauline. I've ignored your mean ways and nasty temper, but I'll not stand for it being directed at my daughter." Dilly paced in their room, shooting contemptuous glances at his wife, who sat in a chair by the window.

"Now, Dilly—"

He held up a hand, stopping whatever else she meant to say. "I've also had enough of your placating tone, Pauline. You know exactly what you're doing and show no remorse for your inappropriate words and actions." Taking out a handkerchief, he wiped it down his face.

"You know I don't really mean—"

"Of course you do!" Feeling his face heat, he stuffed the handkerchief into his pocket, grabbing his hat from the dresser. "I'm going for a drink. When I return, I expect you to have your bags packed."

Jumping to her feet, she stormed toward him. "Why do I need to pack?"

"Because I'm putting you and your son on the stage east tomorrow. When I return home, we'll discuss our marriage and how we can amicably part ways." He didn't wait for her next explosion before leaving for the Dixie.

She almost ran after him before reconsidering. Rubbing her hand over her forehead, Pauline tried to think. Arguing with Dilly now would do no good. He seldom became angry, but when he did, it lasted hours. Sometimes days passed before he calmed enough for a rational conversation.

What she saw tonight scared her. He'd never gone so far as to send her away or mention divorce. Pauline wouldn't mind ending their marriage, but not until she and Oliver secured their future by removing Clare and taking over their inheritance.

Opening the door, she made certain Dilly had left before hurrying to Oliver's room and knocking. "Oliver. Let me in."

The door flew open, her son standing inside with his shirt and shoes off. "What is it?"

Pauline stormed past him, continuing her pacing while rubbing her brow. "It's Dilly. He's sending us home on tomorrow's stage."

"He can't do that." Oliver choked out the words, a deep red creeping up his neck.

Stopping, she glared at him. "Of course he can."

"He'll change his mind by morning and forget all about sending us away."

"Not this time. Dilly meant every word. And he's threatening divorce." She sank into a chair, gripping the arms. "What time does the stage leave for Big Pine?"

"Early afternoon. Why? What are you planning?"

Mouth twisting into a sneer, she narrowed her gaze. "I spoke to Doctor McCord earlier today. He told me Charles plans to work in the clinic tomorrow morning."

"Which means Clare will be alone."

She shot him a feral grin. "An easy target."

Oliver's eyes widened. "You're not thinking of using a gun, are you?"

Pauline shook her head. "Of course I won't be using a gun. *You* will."

"Me? That's ridiculous. Everyone within fifty yards will hear the shot. I'd never make it out of her house before someone came to see what happened."

Standing, she walked to him, gripped his shoulders, and shook him. "Think, Ollie. You're an excellent shot." Dropping her arms, she walked back to the chair.

"With a rifle, not a revolver."

"It doesn't matter. You'll be inside the house. Probably no more than a few feet away from her. It's winter, so the windows will all be closed. And you'll use a pillow to muffle the sound."

"A pillow?" Oliver shot back. "That's outlandish, Mother."

"But it will work, my dear. You hold the pillow in front of the barrel and shoot. What could be easier than that?"

Groaning, he scrubbed a hand down his face. "Poison would be easier and cleaner." He snapped his fingers. "That's it. We'll poison her breakfast."

Blowing out an exasperated breath, Pauline glared at her son. "When? She'll take her breakfast at home with Charles before he leaves for the clinic. Who knows where she'll be at lunch. If Dilly doesn't change his mind, we'll be on the afternoon stage. You have to do it early in the morning after Charles leaves for the clinic."

"But I have no weapon." Oliver's protest had no impact on his mother.

Tapping her lips with a finger, her face brightened. "Dilly has a revolver hidden in our room. You'll use it."

Sagging against a wall, he rubbed the back of his neck. He could think of no further arguments, nothing that would change his mother's mind. She'd nag him until she broke his resolve, the same as she did with anyone who stood in her way. Resigned, he lifted his defeated gaze to her.

"All right, Mother. We might not live through this, but we'll do it your way."

Chapter Twenty-One

Oliver held the gun in a damp hand, hiding in the early morning shadows behind Charles's house. Once the decision had been made the night before, Pauline had hurried to retrieve the revolver and ammunition from its hiding spot before Dilly returned from the saloon. Handing it to her son, she said nothing more before returning to her room and locking the door.

He'd been standing in the bitter cold almost an hour, waiting for Charles to depart for the clinic. If the doctor didn't leave soon, Oliver wouldn't have time to slip into the house, kill Clare, and sneak away before someone spotted him.

His body stiffened, hand tightening on the handle at the sound of a door closing. Peering around the corner, he saw Charles cross the short distance to the back door of the clinic. Heart pounding, Oliver sucked in a deep, fortifying breath, hoping it would help him get through the next few minutes.

The house to the left of Charles's home belonged to Doctor McCord, the one on the right was unoccupied. Behind the house were several unfinished buildings waiting for the warm days of spring to be completed. No one had passed by the entire time Oliver had been posted at the back. There wouldn't be a better time to complete their plans.

Moving slowly along the rear wall, he stopped at the back door, peeking through a nearby window. Clare stood at the wood stove, stirring a pot sitting on top. She paid no attention to anything except the work in front of her.

Gripping the doorknob, he turned it, thankful it didn't squeak a warning. Looking down at the gun in his other hand, he pushed the door open and stepped inside. Clare's back was to him, having no suspicion her life was about to end.

Lifting the gun, he couldn't stop his hand from shaking at the weight of the weapon and the stark fear rippling through him. Placing a finger on the trigger, he began to squeeze, stopping when Clare whirled around to stare at him.

Eyes wide, she opened her mouth to scream when a shot rang out, a sharp pain rocking her backward. Slamming against a wall, she couldn't stop herself from sinking to the floor. Glancing down, she stared in shock at the bright splotch of red spreading over her chest.

Pain scorched through her, blinding her vision as Clare lifted her gaze to stare at the young man standing before her. He looked familiar, but she couldn't recall his name. A smoking gun shook in the hand held limp at his side, a look of horror on his face. She thought he opened his mouth to speak, but couldn't be sure.

Another jolt of pain gripped her. Clare tried to push herself up, but it wasn't to be. Her thoughts went to Charles, their beautiful wedding, the deep love for the man who'd become her husband, and the plans they'd shared. A future she now realized they'd never experience. Sliding into unconsciousness, his name whispered across her lips.

"Charles..."

Panicking, Oliver dropped the gun on the floor, whipping around to dash out the back door. He couldn't breathe, couldn't think. A loud shout sounded in the distance, but he didn't care.

Run, he thought, his boots slogging through ground thick with a mixture of snow and mud.

The pounding sound of boots closed in on him from behind. From the front, people screaming at him to stop had no effect. He continued to run, his only thought of escape.

Before he had time to think further, strong arms banded around his chest, throwing him to the ground. Blinking, he looked up, staring into hard features, piercing eyes the color of molten lead.

"What the hell did you do?" Mack's commanding question and unrelenting stare had Oliver trying to retreat into himself. When he shook his head, Mack grabbed him by the front of his coat, pulled him up, and shoved him at Hex.

Catching Oliver, Hex nodded toward the doc's house. "I've got him. You go help Zeke."

Hex and his brother had been taking their last, early morning walk through town when a shot rang out. A moment later, a man dashed from the Worthington's back door, not stopping at the shouts from the deputies. Hex continued the chase while Zeke ran inside the house.

Slamming open the door, Mack stepped into the kitchen, his gaze landing on Zeke hovered over a woman slumped against a wall. Pressing a hand to the wound on her chest, he looked up at Mack.

"Cash is getting Doc Worthington, but..." Zeke's voice trailed off as he glanced back at Clare, continuing to put pressure on the wound.

Mack knelt beside him. "But?"

Zeke shook his head, not looking up. "It may be too late. Tell me you got the man who did this."

"We did." Mack jumped up, drawing his gun at the sound of the front door crashing open.

"Where is she?" Charles yelled as he walked through the living room toward the kitchen. Seeing blood on the floor and wall, Clare slumped on the floor, he dropped to his knees. Taking in her condition, he shoved Zeke's hands away, replacing them with his own. "See what's taking Clay so long."

An instant later, Clay hurried into the house, carrying his medical bag. Taking in the scene, he moved Mack and Zeke out of the way, dropping to Clare's other side.

"Is the bullet still in her?"

Charles didn't answer, all his concentration on keeping her alive while pressing on the wound.

"Doctor," Clay said louder. "Did the bullet pass through her?"

Swallowing, Charles moved his hand long enough for him to see the bullet still lodged in her chest. "It's still in her, but it looks to be closer to her shoulder."

Opening his bag, Clay removed instruments, a small jar of cerate, and bandages. "I need water and whiskey." He glanced at Charles. "I can handle this if you want to wait in the living room."

A hard glare met Clay's offer. "No. I'm staying." Forcing a calm he didn't feel, Charles stared at Clare. "Let's save her, Doctor."

"I didn't want to do it. It was Mother's idea." Oliver sat on the bed in his cell, hands covering his face as he rocked back and forth. "It's not my fault." Moaning, he looked up, his features drawn, eyes haunted. "It's not even my gun."

Gabe leaned against the wall separating the cells from the front of the jail. Caleb and Mack stood next to him.

"I brought the gun he used, Gabe. It's on your desk." Mack jerked a thumb toward the desk.

Nodding, Gabe walked to the door of the cell. "Whose gun is it?"

"My stepfather's. Dilly Bacon."

Caleb jerked at the name. Stepping next to Gabe, he gripped the bars, his voice low and menacing. "Did Dilly order you to shoot Clare?"

Oliver raised his head, his face a mask of confusion. "I told you. My mother is the one who wanted her killed."

"Pauline?" Caleb asked.

He gave a curt nod. "Yes."

"But why?"

Oliver looked at Caleb, as if seeing him for the first time. "For money, of course."

May sat next to her father in the front part of the jail, listening to Pauline rant and Oliver sob. Caleb stood next to her, his hand resting on her shoulder.

"You do recognize this gun, Mr. Bacon?" Gabe pointed to the six-shooter on his desk.

"Yes. I hadn't known it was missing until Caleb came to tell me what happened." He dragged a hand down his face. "Is Mrs. Worthington going to be all right?"

"We haven't heard." Gabe rested his arms on the desk. "But your wife and stepson better pray she lives."

Rubbing his forehead, Dilly shook his head. "I told Pauline we'd be divorcing once we returned home. Do you think that's why she did this?"

May couldn't help showing her surprise at her father's announcement. "Divorce?"

Reaching over, he took her hand in his. "I never should've married the woman. This trip made it all too clear how unsuitable we are for each other."

"She's a viper, Father."

Dilly lifted a brow. "A viper? Why, yes, May. I do believe that is a good description of her. Although I never expected her to be a part of this." He swept his hand toward the cells, looking at Gabe. "It's hard to believe asking for a divorce would prompt her to kill Mrs. Worthington."

"Oliver said it was about money."

Dilly's brows scrunched together. "How would killing her provide them with money?"

Gabe clenched his hands on the desk, shaking his head in a quick jerk. "I don't know. But I'm going to find out."

Caleb kept his hand on the small of May's back as they walked Dilly back to the hotel. Afterward, they'd stop by the clinic to check on Clare. The only news they'd received indicated Charles and Clay had done what they could and she was still alive.

"Are you sure you don't want me to sit with you, Father?"

Entering the hotel, he took her hand between his two larger ones. "There's no need, sweetheart. I'd rather you find out how Clare is doing and let me know. Please let Charles know I'll do anything I can to help."

"Did you have any idea of the connection between Clare's late husband, Raymond, and your wife's late husband, Harry?" Caleb asked.

"Connection? I'm sorry, but I don't know what you mean."

Nodding toward an alcove in the hotel lobby, Caleb lowered his voice. "Pauline is Harry Billings' widow. His brother, Raymond, is Clare's late husband."

Pinching the bridge of his nose, Dilly shook his head. "I had no idea."

May touched Caleb's arm. "How did you learn of this?"

"Oliver told us before I left to get Dilly. It took a while for us to sort out his ramblings, but we finally figured out what he meant. It still doesn't tell us why he and Pauline wanted to kill Clare. All we know for certain is the shooting was about money."

"I could talk to Pauline. Maybe she'll tell me."

"Thanks, Dilly, but Gabe, Mack, and Dutch will question her and Oliver. If anyone can get them to talk, it's those three." Caleb scanned the lobby, still on watch for Chad Devlin.

Dilly looked between May and Caleb. "I don't believe I've met Dutch."

"He's another deputy. Dutch got back into town not long ago after helping a friend in Denver. He's a former Pinkerton agent and is very good at interrogations."

May worried her bottom lip. "Perhaps Charles and Clare know more, Caleb."

"A good reason for both of you to leave for the clinic. I'll be staying in my room. I need to pack Pauline's and Oliver's belongings. No matter what Gabe learns, those two are out of my life forever."

Leaning up, May kissed her father's check. "I'm so sorry."

"It's odd. When your mother died, I believed I'd lost everything. With Pauline, I don't feel anything at all, except a bit of relief."

May and Caleb watched Dilly walk up the stairs before leaving for the clinic. During their short time in the lobby, it had started to snow, the temperature dropping several degrees. Caleb wrapped an arm around her shoulders, pulling her close as they headed to the clinic.

Once inside, May knocked on the door to one of the examination rooms, holding her breath. When Charles opened it, she and Caleb were stunned to see Clare sitting up in bed.

"You're all right." May brushed past Charles. "We thought..."

"I thought the same when I first saw the wound," Charles said. "There was so much blood, I couldn't get a clear view of the damage. Of course, I was a little upset at the time, which may have added to the way I perceived the injury. Turns out, the bullet lodged in her shoulder. With rest, Clare will be fine in a few weeks."

A broad smile broke across May's face. "That's wonderful news. We've all been so worried about you, Clare. How are you feeling?"

"Very sore. Charles said he could give me laudanum, but I don't like the effects of it. Instead..." She held up a glass with a small amount of whiskey. "I'll sip this when I feel the need." She closed her eyes, leaning back against the pillows.

"I heard they caught the person who shot her."

Caleb gave a terse nod. "He and his mother are in jail."

"His mother?" Charles asked.

"Pauline Bacon. Well, Pauline Billings Bacon."

Clare gasped at Caleb's words. "Billings?"

He nodded. "That was Pauline's married name. Her late husband was Harry Billings."

Clare put a hand over her mouth, her panicked gaze locking on Charles. "Should anything happen to me, Harry's heirs were to get my portion of my late husband's estate."

Caleb rested a hip against the bed. "If you're up to it, perhaps you can tell me everything from the beginning."

May sat on the floor with Isaac, playing with blocks, while Caleb helped Dilly prepare supper. It had been a strange day for all of them.

When Gabe presented the information Caleb had obtained from Clare, Pauline had screamed, pulling her hair while ranting about the Billings family and Dilly. She blamed Clare for taking all the money that should've been hers and Oliver's. Four deputies listened to her ramble, slowly piecing together Pauline's reason for wanting Clare dead. With what they'd heard, she and her son would be in prison a long time.

"Supper is on the table, May."

Caleb's deep voice broke through Isaac's laughter, causing a rush of warmth to curl in her stomach. Inside this house were the three people who meant the most to her. She didn't know what she'd do if she lost any one of them.

Standing, she held out her hand. "Come on, Isaac. Your father has supper ready."

Jumping up, he ran to the table, climbing onto the chair Caleb had carved his name into. May went to pull out her chair, stopping when Caleb beat her to it. Scraping the chair over the wood floor, he waited for her to take a seat.

"This looks wonderful, Caleb."

"Your father did most of the work."

May tilted her head at Dilly. "I didn't know you could cook."

Shrugging, he scooped up a forkful of potatoes. "A man has to eat."

Isaac chattered all through the meal while May and Caleb stole glances at each other. This was what May wanted. Being home every night with Caleb and Isaac, building a future with them, growing a family.

If only Caleb wanted the same.

Chapter Twenty-Two

After supper, Dilly offered to stay with Isaac while Caleb walked May to the boardinghouse. He kept his arm around her shoulders, unwilling to let her get even a few inches away.

As they walked, his gaze moved over the town, his gut sounding a warning he refused to ignore. There'd been no sign of Chad since he'd entered the kitchen and scared May. With no trace of him for several days, most men would believe the outlaw had ridden out of town by now. Caleb knew differently.

Chad had no reason to confront May, unless he meant it as a message for Caleb. The hairs on the back of his neck prickled as they approached the boardinghouse. Picking up the pace, he led her onto the boardwalk and through the front door.

Caleb dropped his arm, turning her toward him. "Stay here. I'll be right back."

"But—"

The door closed before May could get the rest out.

Rushing to the window, she watched Caleb walk across the street toward the livery. With each step, he shifted, glancing one way, then another. Stopping outside the livery, he turned back toward the boardinghouse before walking the short distance to the lumberyard. Again, he stopped, doing the same as outside the livery.

May didn't have to be told whom he sought. Although he'd said nothing, she knew Caleb still worried about the man who'd frightened her. He was certain the man was still in Splendor, even though no one had seen him in several days. She blew out a relieved breath when Caleb walked back toward the boardinghouse, still looking up and down the street. Her heart lurched when he stopped, then ran up the street in the direction of the St. James.

Hurrying outside, May watched, seeing him disappear behind the newly finished church. Chest tightening, she followed, knowing Caleb would chastise her for possibly putting herself in danger. Too bad. She had no intention of letting him walk into a dangerous situation alone.

Before she reached the church, Caleb came around the other side, muttering a curse when he spotted her. Stopping a few inches away, he placed fisted hands on his hips.

"What do you think you're doing, leaving the boardinghouse when I told you to stay?"

She'd never heard his voice this cold, his face twisted in anger. May's anger rose as well, but she forced herself to remain calm.

"I was worried about you."

"So you just ran outside, not thinking how you might be putting yourself in danger?" His breathing was hard, his tone shifting from anger to disgust. Or was it concern?

Swallowing, she took a step toward him, reaching out to rest her palm against his chest. "I saw you run up the street. It scared me, so I followed." Searching the lines of worry on his face, she leaned up, kissing his chin. "Were you looking for the man who came into the kitchen?"

"Ah hell, May."

Placing a hand on the small of her back, he took quick steps toward the St. James, his gaze still searching the area. Guiding her inside, he headed straight to the desk.

"Good evening, Thomas."

"Hello, Deputy Covington, Miss Bacon. Are you here for supper?"

"Actually, I'd like a room for May. One near her father, if that's possible."

"Certainly." Thomas ran a finger down the guest list. "Let me see what we have."

Gripping his arm, May tugged him away from the desk. "What do you think you're doing?"

"Trying to keep you safe."

"I'm safe at the boardinghouse, Caleb."

"You'll be safer here, May. Which means I'll sleep better."

"Deputy. We have a room right next to Mr. Bacon."

"Thanks, Thomas." Bending over the register, Caleb signed his name, paid for the room, and palmed the key. "Do you have an extra key to her room?"

Thomas's brow shot up. "Well, yes. We always keep two extra for each room."

Caleb held out his hand. "I'll take one of them. And to answer your question, no, I am not staying with May." A grin tipped his lips at the shock on Thomas's face. Turning, he took May's arm.

"I don't want you paying for a room, Caleb. It's too expensive and I don't need it." She tried to tug her arm free, feeling his grip tighten. "Darn you."

Chuckling, he led her up the stairs. "Such language, Miss Bacon." He ignored her derisive snort, escorting her to a room next to her father's. Unlocking the door, he looked around, then guided her inside. "Stay here and do not leave. I'll ask Suzanne to pack some of your clothes. Tomorrow is Sunday. I'll be here with Isaac to escort you to church."

Hands clenched in front of her, May stared at him as if he were mad. "You can't force me to stay here. I'll not allow you to order me around because of some whim."

"*Whim?*" Caleb shouted, fisted hands on his hips. "Do you know why I ran up the street tonight?"

Lifting her face, she jutted out her chin. "No, but I—"

His next words cut off whatever else she meant to say. "Because I'm certain the man who frightened you was watching us. He stood in the shadows, and by your description, I've no doubt of his identity. He watched us from the livery until we reached the boardinghouse. I lost him for a bit, then saw him again near the church. That's when I ran up the street."

Crossing her arms, she glared up at him. "Why didn't you tell me?"

"And what would you have done?" He saw the instant his words registered, dropping his hands to his sides. Caleb didn't want her to know the man's true identity or his possible reason for being in Splendor. It would only scare her further. Voice softening, he took her hands in his. "This is my job, May. Until I know he means you no harm or he leaves town, I need to know you're safe."

Shoulders slumping under his pleading gaze, she let out a breath. "All right, Caleb. But I don't want to stay here more than a couple nights."

Leaning down, he brushed a kiss across her lips. "You may grow to like it. It's certainly more convenient to get to work. Just walk down the back stairs and you'll be in the kitchen."

"With Christmas on Wednesday, I don't return to work until Thursday. Gary offered to prepare food for the hotel guests. Lena doesn't expect there to be many, so he won't need my help in the kitchen."

"Good. Then I'll know where you'll be."

She lifted her chin again. "I am not staying in this room for four days, Caleb."

"You're right. You'll be with me."

Caleb stood with Gabe, several deputies, and Dom outside church, his gaze fixed on May. She held Isaac's hand while speaking with Sylvia and a few other women. Church had ended ten minutes earlier, and he'd wasted no time calling the men together.

"You're certain it was Devlin you saw last night, Caleb?"

"Not a doubt in my mind, Gabe. He never left town."

"And he's been watching you and May," Hex added, scanning the crowd, the same as the other men. "The poster says he's still wanted for murder and robbing more than one stage."

Gabe's gaze found Lena in the group of women, knowing how he'd feel if anyone came after his wife. "We need to find him."

Cash rubbed his chin while he watched Allie talking with May. He looked at Gabe. "There's a quick way to find him."

Caleb watched a look pass between the two men, jaw clenching when he understood. "Absolutely not. We're *not* using May as bait to draw Devlin to us."

"Think about it, Caleb." Gabe narrowed his gaze on him. "When Devlin is ready to make a move, he'll want you to know it's him. That means he'll come out in the open. When he does, we'll be ready."

Dragging a hand down his face, he shook his head. "No. There has to be another way."

Mack stepped next to him. "Tell us what it is. This is your decision to make, Caleb."

Massaging the back of his neck, he blew out a breath. "I don't have another idea."

Seeing Noah standing near the church with Abby and their son, Gabe motioned him over. Waiting until his friend stood next to him, Gabe described his plan.

"Noah and Dom will be included. Noah will take a position upstairs in one of the buildings. Caleb, you and May will stay within a specific area between your house and the St. James, making it easier for the rest of us to keep you safe. Devlin will want to approach you at night when it'll be easier for him to keep his identity secret. As a precaution during the day, May will need to stay inside or venture out only if she's with several other people." Gabe glanced around the circle of men. "I want this finished before Christmas."

"If anything happens to her..." Caleb's words faded at the unthinkable.

Noah placed a hand on his shoulder. "We won't let it."

Caleb sat with May, Isaac, and Dilly in the Eagle's Nest early Sunday afternoon, doing all he could to hide his agitation. Gabe's plan would start this evening, but he still hadn't come to terms with putting May in danger.

Caleb had spoken to her father privately about the threat to May. He'd been taken aback when Dilly grabbed his arm, threatening death if anything happened to his daughter. Caleb understood the man's fear. He felt it himself.

After their early supper, the four took a slow turn around town, ending at Caleb's house. As planned, Dilly offered to watch Isaac so he and May could have some time alone. This meant another walk using a specific route, with Gabe, all his deputies, and Noah posted around.

Caleb not only hated the added danger to May, but the fact they weren't alone. He couldn't hold or kiss her, relax and talk of their possible future knowing numerous men watched over them. After an hour, he escorted May to the hotel, leaving within minutes to relieve Dilly.

Monday passed quietly, Caleb taking May and Isaac for a brief buggy ride. The cold wind chilled them as he drove north toward the Pelletier ranch, then turned back when a new wave of snow began to fall. At least the freezing temperature kept the road solid, avoiding the wheels being sucked into the mud, as would happen after a couple days of sun.

They repeated the same routine as the night before, taking a walk but still not drawing Chad out into the open. By Tuesday, Caleb's patience had run out and guilt plagued him. He hadn't been honest with May about her part in exposing Chad. She didn't even know his name or his prior connection to Caleb.

Sitting across the desk from Gabe, he'd been prepared to call off another night of what seemed a wasted effort when the door crashed open and Dom walked inside.

"Devlin is camped to the northeast, just outside town. I saw him when I rode out to check some property I'm thinking of buying."

"You're certain it was Devlin?" Caleb asked.

"No doubt. By the time I circled around to come up behind him, he'd ridden off. The tracks showed him riding south toward Splendor."

Gabe leaned forward. "Which means he might be planning something for tonight."

Dom gave a curt nod. "The fact we didn't spot him the last two nights doesn't mean he wasn't here, watching Caleb and May, figuring out how to get to them." He glanced between Gabe and Caleb. "I'm certain he'll make his move tonight."

Pursing his lips, Gabe rocked back in his chair, jerking his thumb toward the door. "Caleb, find Mack, Cash, Beau, and the others. I'll let Noah know we believe tonight is when Devlin will appear."

Caleb tightened his grip on May's hand as they left his house to walk between the buildings. As in the previous two nights, they'd stay to the south end of town, taking their time as they passed the closed shops, the Dixie, and the St. James before crossing the street to start the route over again.

Other than saying their hellos to people they recognized, the first turn around town was uneventful. Caleb thought the second round would be the same until the hairs on the back of his neck prickled. Slowing his pace, he let go of May's hand, unbuttoning his coat to expose his gun before draping his arm over her shoulders.

Looking up at the window in the second floor of the St. James, he spotted Noah's silhouette. The other men were inside shops or hidden behind large, wooden barrels between the buildings. He knew Cash would be in the apartment above his wife's millinery, his rifle poised and ready.

Crossing the street, he stayed vigilant. The instincts telling him to get her into the St. James and out of danger warred with the need to stay calm and focus.

"I'll bet you thought you'd never see me again, Covington." The raspy voice he recognized came from behind them. Turning, he didn't see Devlin. Moving his hand to the handle of his six-shooter, he pushed May behind him.

"Come out and show yourself, Devlin. No need to hide like the coward you are."

He heard a scornful laugh an instant before Chad stepped out the door of the original clinic to the edge of the boardwalk, his gun pointed at Caleb. "I'd say that description fits you a helluva lot better than me. I mean, you're the one who shot my brothers in the back when they ran."

He felt May's arms go around him from behind, her head resting against his back. "What does he mean, Caleb?"

Ignoring her question, Caleb took a quick glance down the street, seeing Mack standing in one doorway, Hex in another.

"Don't move until I tell you to, May." Caleb bit out the request, hoping she'd do what he asked.

"Why don't you introduce me to your pretty lady, Deputy?"

Caleb stiffened. "I believe you've already met her, Chad."

The outlaw's features twisted into a menacing grin. "Maybe I did. I'd still like a formal introduction. I assume you've already told her all about me."

"Come out onto the street and I'll think about it."

The feral laugh didn't surprise Caleb. "Well, now, I'm thinking this spot right here is just fine."

Out of the corner of his eye, he spotted movement in front of the gunsmith shop. Not wanting to take his attention off Chad, Caleb didn't risk a look. A few seconds later, he saw Mack and Hex walk into the street, their guns drawn. He knew Cash would have a good shot, but doubted Noah could see Devlin.

"Hey there, Deputy." Caleb startled at Enoch Weaver's familiar, slurred voice. "I see you have your lady with you tonight." Coming up to stand in front of Caleb, Enoch whipped his tattered hat from his head and bowed. "Good evening, miss. I don't believe I've had the pleasure." His garbled voice had May taking a quick look around Caleb.

Wincing at the smell of sour whiskey, unwashed clothes, and body odor, Caleb didn't take his gaze off Chad. "May, don't move. Enoch, why don't you head over to the Dixie and we'll meet you there in a bit?"

Enoch shook his head in a frantic gesture, waving toward the Dixie. "I think it would be a marvelous idea if you two came with me. We can all have drinks and talk—"

"What the hell is going on over there, Covington?" Chad stepped onto the street, his gun still pointed at Caleb.

Whipping around, Enoch teetered before reclaiming his balance and walking straight toward the outlaw. Settling his hat back on his head, he extended his hand. "I'm Enoch Weaver."

"I don't give a damn who you are. Get out of the way before you get shot." Chad kept his gaze on Enoch, not noticing the deputies moving up behind him or the others positioned nearby.

Shaking his head again, Enoch continued forward, staggering a little. "Ah, now. You wouldn't shoot an old man like me, or the nice deputy and his lady."

"I'm warning you, old man. Get out of the way." Chad shifted his aim to point the gun at Enoch.

"No need to get angry." Enoch's face broke into a tight grin.

"Enoch, get out of the way."

269

The drunk heard Caleb's voice, ignoring it.

Nostrils flaring, Chad's deadly eyes locked on Enoch. "You were warned."

"Enoch, get down!"

Before anyone could react, Enoch pulled a gun and fired, putting a bullet in the middle of Chad's forehead. Taking the last few steps, he stared down at the fallen man, shaking his head before turning back to Caleb and shrugging.

"All I wanted was to introduce myself." Sliding the gun into the hidden holster, Enoch staggered off the street and into the Dixie.

Caleb paced the lobby of the St. James on Christmas Eve. After last night, fearing he might lose May, he'd made a decision. He'd already spoken with Reverend Paige, Dilly, Gabe, and Mack, leaving the most important conversation for last. Hearing May's light laughter, he looked up, seeing her come downstairs on the arm of her father.

Dilly walked up, extending his hand, a knowing look in his eyes. "Good evening, Caleb."

He gripped the offered hand. "Mr. Bacon." Swallowing, his gaze shifted to May. "Good morning, May."

"Hello, Caleb."

Dilly deftly moved his daughter next to Caleb, slipping her arm through his. "Are we all ready for the Christmas service?"

Smiling up at Caleb, May nodded. "I believe we are, Father."

A few minutes later, they entered the newly finished church, sharing a row with Mack, Sylvia, and Dom. After several hymns and the message, Reverend Paige put his notes aside and looked out onto the crowd.

"Before I excuse you to enjoy your Christmas, I've received a special request." His gaze landed on Caleb. "Deputy Covington."

Chest constricting so much he had a hard time drawing a breath, Caleb stood. Last night, his idea seemed perfect. This morning, he wasn't so certain. Shoving aside his doubts, he extended a hand to May, drawing her up to stand next to him. The moment she straightened, he dropped to one knee, eliciting a gasp not only from May, but from several others.

"May Bacon, I've been a blind fool long enough. I love you. Have for a long time." He paused a moment, seeing moisture in her eyes. Blowing out a ragged breath, he continued. "I know we've had some problems, and you've put up with a lot from me. Even with all that, I'm hoping you'll excuse my failings and agree to be my wife."

Unable to speak without bursting into tears, she nodded frantically while swiping moisture from her face.

Standing, the corners of Caleb's mouth tilted upward into a broad smile. "Is that a yes?"

Nodding again, she launched herself into his arms. "It's definitely a yes."

Epilogue

The following Saturday…

Caleb's heart stilled as he watched May walk down the church aisle in a dress Allie created over the last two days. In her hands she held a bough of pine decorated with sprigs of holly. The smile on her face sliced right through him, causing his chest to squeeze. He'd never seen anyone more beautiful.

The ceremony passed in a blur. Before Caleb realized it, he held May in his arms, brushing a kiss across her lips. "I love you, May."

"I love you, too, Caleb."

Turning them around, he held up their joined hands to the congratulations and joyous shouts from the guests. A few minutes later, chairs had been pushed to the side and tables set up, allowing Suzanne, Gary, and several other women to set out a wide array of food and drinks along one wall. In one corner, three men played music, encouraging the guests to get out in the middle of the floor and dance. In another corner, May and Caleb, both still reeling from the events of the past week, stood with her father and several friends.

"Did anyone know Enoch was a retired U.S. Marshal?" Dom lifted a glass of punch to his lips, grimacing at the thick, sweet taste.

"Perhaps this will help." Nick held out a flask, shielding Dom from the rest of the crowd while he poured a small amount into his glass. Taking another sip, he grinned.

"Thanks, Nick. That's much better. Back to my question about Enoch."

Gabe shook his head, as did Mack and Hex.

"The man may spend a lot of time with a glass of whiskey in his hand, but he's a mighty fine shot." Nick tilted his glass toward Enoch, who'd wandered inside to congratulate Caleb and May. "I do believe we owe him a dinner at the Eagle's Nest. Don't you, Gabe?"

"I do." He watched his friend's gaze settle on a couple across the room. "When are you going to let Clay know you have no issue with him courting Olivia?"

Nick grinned. "Just seeing how long it will take for him to show some spunk and force the issue. I don't want my daughter marrying a man who won't fight for her."

"From what I know, you're not going to get a fight from the doctor, Nick. He's as calm as any man I've ever met." Dom lifted his glass again, looking over the rim at the woman standing next to Olivia. He'd been attracted to Josephine Dubois from the moment she'd stepped off the stage, smiled, and dashed into Olivia's open arms. The uninhibited, spontaneous scene had stuck with him. Now all he could think about was getting to know Olivia's best friend.

"Did you hear back from Washington about the Marshal position, Dom?"

Tearing his gaze away from Josephine, he looked at Gabe. "A telegram came yesterday saying I'd been accepted. Neil Howie is going to ride over from Big Pine next week to administer the oath."

Hex clasped him on the shoulder. "That's great news. Will you be moving to Big Pine?"

Dom gave a crisp shake of his head. "Nope. Staying here was a condition of my application. Doesn't mean I won't be traveling a lot, though. I'd appreciate it if all of you would witness the oath."

"Does that mean you won't be buying the property?" Mack asked.

"I'm buying the land. By the time Howie gets here, I'll be the owner of enough land to run some cattle and have a few horses." His gaze wandered back to Josephine, who was now talking and laughing with Hex's brother, Zeke.

"Why don't you go over and ask her to dance?" Hex took a draw from his flask, slipping it back into a pocket when Dom declined a sip. "Zeke can't dance a lick. My guess is the pretty young woman from New Orleans can."

Feeling a strong hand clasp his shoulder, Dom stiffened, realizing it belonged to Nick.

"You be real careful with what you do about Josephine. The same as Olivia, she's a sweet, naïve girl without experience and from a real strict upbringing. I wouldn't want to call you out, Dom."

Jaw tightening, he absorbed the warning. "I understand your meaning, Nick."

Dom already suspected everything Nick said about Josephine, deciding nothing would keep him away from the enticing southern beauty. Unlike Clay, Dom knew how to fight for what he wanted. And he definitely wanted Josephine Dubois.

Thank you for taking the time to read Angel Peak. If you enjoyed it, please consider telling your friends or posting a short review. Word of mouth is an author's best friend and much appreciated.

Watch for book nine in the Redemption Mountain series, Restless Wind.

Please join my reader's group to be notified of my New Releases at:
https://www.shirleendavies.com/contact-me.html

I care about quality, so if you find something in error, please contact me via email at
shirleen@shirleendavies.com

About the Author

Shirleen Davies writes romance—historical and contemporary western romance with a touch of suspense. She is the best-selling author of the MacLarens of Fire Mountain Series, the MacLarens of Boundary Mountain Series, and the Redemption Mountain Series. Shirleen grew up in Southern California, attended Oregon State University, and has degrees from San Diego State University and the University of Maryland. Her passion is writing emotionally charged stories of flawed people who find redemption through love and acceptance. She lives with her husband in a beautiful town in northern Arizona. Between them, they have five adult sons who are their greatest achievements.

I love to hear from my readers!

Send me an email: shirleen@shirleendavies.com
Visit my Website: www.shirleendavies.com
Sign up to be notified of New Releases:
www.shirleendavies.com
Check out all of my Books:
www.shirleendavies.com/books.html
Comment on my Blog:
www.shirleendavies.com/blog.html
Follow me on Amazon:
http://www.amazon.com/author/shirleendavies

Follow my on BookBub:
https://www.bookbub.com/authors/shirleen-davies

Other ways to connect with me:

Facebook Author Page:
http://www.facebook.com/shirleendaviesauthor
Twitter: www.twitter.com/shirleendavies
Pinterest: http://pinterest.com/shirleendavies
Instagram:
https://www.instagram.com/shirleendavies_author/
Google Plus:
https://plus.google.com/+ShirleenDaviesAuthor

Books by Shirleen Davies
Historical Western Romance Series
MacLarens of Fire Mountain

Tougher than the Rest, Book One
Faster than the Rest, Book Two
Harder than the Rest, Book Three
Stronger than the Rest, Book Four
Deadlier than the Rest, Book Five
Wilder than the Rest, Book Six

Redemption Mountain

Redemption's Edge, Book One
Wildfire Creek, Book Two
Sunrise Ridge, Book Three
Dixie Moon, Book Four
Survivor Pass, Book Five
Promise Trail, Book Six
Deep River, Book Seven
Courage Canyon, Book Eight
Forsaken Falls, Book Nine
Solitude Gorge, Book Ten
Rogue Rapids, Book Eleven
Restless Wind, Coming next in the series!

MacLarens of Boundary Mountain

Colin's Quest, Book One,

Brodie's Gamble, Book Two
Quinn's Honor, Book Three
Sam's Legacy, Book Four
Heather's Choice, Book Five
Nate's Destiny, Book Six
Blaine's Wager, Book Seven
Fletcher's Pride, Book Eight
Bay's Desire, Coming next in the series!

Contemporary Romance Series

MacLarens of Fire Mountain

Second Summer, Book One
Hard Landing, Book Two
One More Day, Book Three
All Your Nights, Book Four
Always Love You, Book Five
Hearts Don't Lie, Book Six
No Getting Over You, Book Seven
'Til the Sun Comes Up, Book Eight
Foolish Heart, Book Nine
Forever Love, Book Ten, Coming next in the series!

Peregrine Bay

Reclaiming Love, Book One, A Novella
Our Kind of Love, Book Two

Burnt River

Shane's Burden, Book One by Peggy Henderson
Thorn's Journey, Book Two by Shirleen Davies
Aqua's Achilles, Book Three by Kate Cambridge
Ashley's Hope, Book Four by Amelia Adams
Harpur's Secret, Book Five by Kay P. Dawson
Mason's Rescue, Book Six by Peggy L. Henderson
Del's Choice, Book Seven by Shirleen Davies
Ivy's Search, Book Eight by Kate Cambridge
Phoebe's Fate, Book Nine by Amelia Adams
Brody's Shelter, Book Ten by Kay P. Dawson
Boone's Surrender, Book Eleven by Shirleen Davies
Watch for more books in the series!

The best way to stay in touch is to subscribe to my newsletter. Go to www.shirleendavies.com and subscribe in the box at the top of the right column that asks for your email. You'll be notified of new books before they are released, have chances to win great prizes, and receive other subscriber-only specials.

Avalanche Ranch Press, LLC
PO Box 12618
Prescott, AZ 86304

Angel Peak is a work of fiction. Names, characters, places, and incidents are either products of the author's imagination or used fictitiously. Any resemblance to actual events, locales, or persons, living or dead, is wholly coincidental.

Made in the USA
Middletown, DE
04 April 2023

28220830R00175